Heartland

Sooner or Later

Heartland

❧

Share every moment . . .

Heartland

~

Sooner or Later

by **Lauren Brooke**

SCHOLASTIC INC.

New York Toronto London Auckland Sydney
Mexico City New Delhi Hong Kong Buenos Aires

No part of this publication may be reproduced in whole or in part, or stored in a retrieval system, or transmitted in any form or by any means, electronic, mechanical, photocopying, recording, or otherwise, without written permission of the publisher. For information regarding permission, write to Scholastic Inc., Attention: Permissions Department, 557 Broadway, New York, NY 10012.

ISBN 0-439-33968-5

Heartland series created by Working Partners Ltd, London.

Copyright © 2003 by Working Partners Ltd.
Published by Scholastic Inc. All rights reserved.

SCHOLASTIC and associated logos are trademarks and/or registered trademarks of Scholastic Inc. HEARTLAND is a trademark and/or registered trademark of Working Partners Ltd.

12 11 10 9 8 7 6 5 4 3 2   3 4 5 6 7 8/0
Printed in the U.S.A.   40
First Scholastic printing, June 2003

With special thanks to Linda Chapman

To Tan and Bramble, my two special boys.
I couldn't have written this book if I hadn't had
to say good-bye to you, but if I'd had the choice . . .

This book is also dedicated to Mark Rashid
for his amazing books on working with horses
and to Nick, Brian, and everyone else at Meadow
Lane Veterinary Centre for answering my
questions so patiently. Any mistakes are mine,
but there are many scenes in Heartland that
could not have been written without their help.
Thank you.

Chapter One

At five o'clock, Amy's alarm clock rang out. Surfacing from a dream, she groped for the off button. It couldn't be time to get up yet, could it? She flopped back against her pillows and shut her eyes. *Just a few more minutes*, she thought.

She woke with a start sometime later. What time was it? She looked at her clock. Quarter to six! She was never going to be ready to leave by eight!

Quickly, she jumped out of bed and grabbed her jeans from the floor. She pulled on her clothes and, tying her long light-brown hair back in a ponytail, she ran down the stairs and outside.

Brush Storm. Braid him. Put his show trunk in Ben's trailer. Muck out six stalls. The list of things to do ran through her mind. Looking over her horse's door, her heart sank.

In the night, Storm's sheet had slipped, and he now had a large manure stain on his near flank.

"Oh, why do I have a gray horse!" Amy groaned.

Getting some water and a grooming kit, she set to work on cleaning him up.

As soon as he was looking respectable again, Amy started on the stalls. She finished Dylan's in half the time it usually took and, grabbing the wheelbarrow handles, she began to take the dirty straw up to the muck heap, half running to save time.

Just before she got there, the barrow wheel hit a stone. Amy lost her grip on the handles, and the load toppled to one side, spilling dirty straw and droppings all over the yard.

"Oh, great!" Amy shouted in frustration.

"Having fun?"

Amy swung around.

Ben Stillman, one of Heartland's stable hands and Amy's friend, was grinning at her. She'd been so busy she hadn't heard him arrive. "You know, most people wait until they get to the muck heap before they tip the wheelbarrow, Amy," he commented, an amused look on his face.

"Not funny!" Amy exclaimed.

Luckily, Ben realized that she didn't need teasing that morning. "Hey, come on," he said easily. "I'll help you clean it up."

Grabbing a broom, he started to sweep the dirty straw into a pile. "Having a bad morning?" he said.

"You could say that," Amy said despairingly. "I still haven't braided Storm. I overslept."

"It's not surprising, the hours you've been putting in recently," Ben commented. "Relax. I'll braid Storm for you after I've done Red."

"Thanks, Ben," Amy said, feeling a weight drop from her shoulders. "I'll owe you one."

"I know," Ben said with a grin. "Just you wait." He put the broom away, and they went back down the yard together. "You know, I'm sure Ty wouldn't mind doing the extra stalls on a show morning," he said as they walked to the front stable block, with its white-painted doors and hanging baskets full of flowers. "Why don't you ask him?"

A smile lifted the corners of Amy's lips as she thought about Ty, who was Heartland's main stable hand and her boyfriend. "He's already offered," she told Ben. "But I feel bad enough going off to shows and leaving him to work all the horses. It wouldn't seem fair, getting him to do my share of the stalls, too." She shrugged. "I can cope."

"If you don't oversleep," Ben said dryly.

"Yes — if," Amy said with a grin.

By seven o'clock, she had finished four stalls and was sweeping up in front of them. Seeing Ty's pickup turning into the driveway, Amy's heart turned in her chest. Since they'd started dating a few months ago, they'd had their ups and downs, but things were going really well between them now. Ty helped Amy treat the horses at Heartland while Lou, Amy's older sister, organized the business side of things, and Jack, the girls' grandfather, helped out by doing maintenance on the farm and running the house.

"Mornin'," Ty said, getting out of the truck and heading over. He glanced around at the tidy yard. "You seem very organized," he said, looking impressed.

"You should have seen it an hour ago," Amy confessed. "It was anything but organized then, but Ben's been helping me. I've mucked out four of the stalls in the front block and done all the watering."

"Great," Ty said, kissing her. "I'll go and do the feeds."

While Ty gave the horses their breakfast, Amy distributed the hay nets, finished the two remaining stalls in the front block, and then loaded her show gear into Ben's black trailer. Finally, she led Storm into the trailer beside Red. "I can't believe it's only eight o'clock," she said as she and Ben got into the pickup. "It already feels like the middle of the day." She sank back into the seat and looked out the window as Ben started the engine.

She had a whole hour now to do nothing while Ben drove them to the show. Bliss!

But even though her body was able to relax, her mind couldn't. She kept thinking about Heartland and all the horses that needed working. Luckily, both she and Ben were in early classes. They should be back in time to help Ty in the afternoon. Things were so busy at Heartland! Amy's best friend, Soraya, usually helped out, but she was away at camp for the rest of the summer — and having a great time if her e-mails were any indication.

Amy ran through the horses in her mind. There was Dylan, the clumsy young show jumper in the stall next to Storm. Then there was Solitaire, a headstrong yearling that was at Heartland to learn some manners. They both needed a training session that day. And then there was Willow, a new pony that was terrified of people. They hadn't even started working with her yet. And Sundance, Amy's pony. He was recovering from a strained tendon and would soon be ready for some light riding. There was certainly a lot for Amy to do.

"You're quiet," Ben commented, interrupting her thoughts.

"I'm just thinking about everything there is to do back home," Amy told him.

"Well, don't," Ben said firmly. "Right now you should be thinking about the show — and Storm."

"I know. It's just that . . ." Amy's voice trailed off. It was difficult to explain. She loved taking Storm to shows. She loved the buzz, the excitement. But it wasn't easy leaving Heartland behind. There were so many horses there who needed her love and attention. She glanced at Ben. He wouldn't be able to understand. He liked working at Heartland, but it wasn't his passion — he lived for taking Red on the show circuit. "It doesn't matter," she said quietly.

"So, you're focused on the show now, right?" Ben ordered.

"Yes." Amy smiled, pushing Heartland out of her mind. "I'm focused on the show."

By the time they arrived, the competition was already well under way. The short-stirrup and lead line classes were finishing up. Horses were in the schooling ring and grooms hurried about with brushes and rags in hand.

While Ben went to the secretary's tent to sign in and collect their numbers, Amy saddled up Storm. Her class, the Junior Jumpers, was scheduled to start shortly in the second ring.

"Here," Ben said, coming back and handing Amy her number. "It looks like everything is running on time. They said you should be able to walk the course in about ten minutes."

"Great," said Amy, gathering up her reins. "I'll go and start warming up."

She found a quiet spot behind the trailers. She liked to have some time alone with Storm before she took him into one of the busy practice rings.

As she rode around on a loose rein, Amy felt herself relaxing. Storm was a joy to ride. Sensitive and well schooled, he obeyed her lightest signal. Most of the horses at Heartland had come from upsetting circum-stances and demanded every ounce of brainpower and concentration that Amy had. She needed to anticipate how they would respond to any given situation. But Storm had never been treated badly, and Amy knew just what to expect from him. She patted his neck. He was one of the lucky ones.

"Amy!" It was Ben, calling her and pointing at his watch. "Time to walk the course!"

She was relieved to have Ben there to keep her on track. He held Storm while she went into the ring. The brightly painted fences looked solid and big — they were just under four feet, but Amy didn't feel intimi-dated. Storm could jump them easily. She walked up to each fence, working out where she should steady Storm and where she should push him forward. It was a timed first-round class, meaning the horses that jumped clear immediately started the jump-off course, which would be run against the clock. It was a test of the horse's endurance and of the rider's composure. Remembering the two courses wouldn't be easy.

As Amy reached the second-to-last jump, a big red wall, she stopped. On the other side of the wall, a slim girl with long blond hair was assessing the distance to the same fence. It was Ashley Grant. Amy took a deep breath. She and Ashley had quite a history.

Ashley's mother, Val Grant, owned a highly successful hunter-jumper barn called Green Briar. Although the Green Briar horses and ponies were consistently winning top ribbons, Amy was skeptical of Val's harsh training methods. And when Ashley's flashy new show jumper, Bright Magic, had started acting up, Ashley had secretly asked Amy for help. Amy had reluctantly agreed to watch Ashley and give some suggestions of ways to counter Magic's bad habits. Amy's techniques were completely contrary to those Ashley's mother used, and they were extremely effective. Nonetheless, Amy was left feeling betrayed and used when Ashley turned her back on Amy's sound advice and returned to riding in the strict, crop-heavy style Val Grant preferred.

Amy didn't want to speak to Ashley, and she was about to walk away without a word when she heard her name.

"Amy!" Ashley called, her cheeks flushing slightly.

Just for a moment, Ashley seemed to hesitate, but

then her eyes hardened into their usual cool expression. "It's good you're taking your time looking at this jump, Amy," she said, flashing a coy smile. "It's bound to cause problems for you and Storm."

"Sorry?" Amy said, raising her eyebrows. She folded her arms, uncertain what to make of Ashley's vague insult. "I think we'll do fine. Just a reminder, Ashley, but we did beat you last time."

"Fluke," Ashley said coldly.

"Really?" Amy said in disbelief. "Well, I guess we'll see what happens in the ring today, then."

A strident voice rang out. "Ashley!"

Val Grant was standing by the ring entrance, frowning. "Hurry up!" she shouted to Ashley. "Magic still needs warming up!"

"See you when I ride into the ring to claim the blue ribbon," Ashley said as she marched away across the ring.

"So what was on Ashley's mind?" Ben asked when Amy returned to him and Storm.

"Just more of her usual condescending threats," Amy said, shaking her head. "I can't believe I helped her with Magic. I really thought she wanted to change. But she's the same as ever."

"It can't be easy having a mom like hers," Ben said slowly.

Amy looked across to where Val Grant was giving Ashley a pep talk. "They're a perfect pair," she said, but she knew Ben was right.

"Forget about them." Ben touched her arm. "You should be concentrating on Storm — and the courses."

"You're right." Pushing all thoughts of the Grants out of her mind, Amy mounted and rode Storm into the warm-up ring.

Val Grant was walking toward one of the practice jumps. She was shouting at her daughter, who was now mounted on Bright Magic.

"Use your crop! Take hold of his mouth! Show him you mean business!"

Amy took Storm down to the other end of the ring and worked him until he was relaxed and really listening to her, then she turned him toward the practice fence. Val Grant was still standing next to it, one hand idly slapping a crop against her leather riding boots. When Storm was just a few strides from the jump, he saw the crop rise and fall and spooked slightly, taking off too close and catching the pole with his front legs.

He shot off after the jump, shaking his head.

"He's going to have to jump cleaner than that in the ring, Amy," Val Grant called as she put the pole back up. "He could be a good horse if you got after him and taught him a lesson or two."

"Like I'm going to take advice from you," Amy muttered under her breath as she struggled to bring Storm back under control. What was with the Grants and their mock friendship? Slowing Storm to a trot, she circled him until she felt him relax again. Seeing the approach to the jump was free, she widened her canter circle and popped him cleanly over the fence with no fuss.

Val Grant nodded.

Patting Storm, Amy slowed him to a walk. There were four horses before them. She'd let him have a short rest now.

As she walked Storm around the outside of the practice ring, she kept one eye on the showring. The announcer called for Ashley and Bright Magic. Amy halted Storm and watched. How would Magic jump? He'd looked agitated in the practice ring. When Amy had worked with him and Ashley, she had quickly realized that the horse was very sensitive. When he was ridden quietly, he jumped well, but if he was pushed and pressured, he tended to panic. Amy had suggested Ashley ride him in a snaffle bit without a crop, and he had responded beautifully. Still, at the last show, Ashley had returned to her old ways — her mom's ways. She had used her crop, and Magic had panicked and jumped poorly. Amy watched curiously. How would Ashley ride him today?

To her relief, she saw Ashley loosen the reins of her double bridle as soon as she was away from her mom.

Bright Magic lowered his head slightly and seemed to relax. When the starting bell rang, Ashley fumbled with her crop. It fell to the ground, but Ashley didn't stop to get it. Stroking Magic's neck, she headed him toward the first jump, a smile flickering across her face.

She's done it on purpose, Amy thought. *She meant to drop it.*

Calm now that the crop was gone, Magic jumped the first fence perfectly.

"Good." Amy breathed. She caught herself. She was competing against Magic. She shouldn't be rooting for him! But deep down, she knew that she cared about Magic's welfare more than the competition. She'd rather see him happy than stressed out and misunderstood. And if that meant he and Ashley might beat Amy and Storm, so be it.

Ashley and Magic jumped both the initial course and the jump-off clear and rode out to the sound of applause. As Ashley left the ring, she passed Amy.

Amy hesitated, but then, remembering the way Ashley had dropped the crop, decided to be civil. "Good round, Ashley," she called.

"Thanks," Ashley said briefly without slowing. She rode over to her mom.

Val Grant, all smiles now, congratulated Ashley. Seeing Amy watching, she smiled smugly. "You're going to have to go some way to beat that, young lady," she called out. "Isn't she, Ashley?"

Ashley nodded, avoiding Amy's eyes.

Amy turned Storm away. "Just watch me try," she muttered. Setting her chin, she gathered up her reins. "Come on, Storm," she whispered. "Let's show everyone what we can do."

Amy cantered Storm into the ring. While she was relieved that Ashley had ridden Magic well, she was now consumed with a sense of competition. She had never felt so determined to beat anyone in her life. Seeming to sense her determination, Storm's ears pricked. The starting bell rang out, and they were off. Jump after jump flowed beneath them. They finished the first part of the course, and Amy heard the bell ring, indicating that she should continue.

She touched Storm's neck with her fingertips. "Let's go for it," she whispered as they passed the timing post.

Storm flew over the jumps, cutting corners to trim seconds from their time. As they cantered through the finish to the sound of applause, Amy listened for the loudspeaker. It crackled into life.

"A double clear there for Amy Fleming on Summer Storm," the announcer said.

Amy looked at the clock and felt a surge of pride. She'd done it! She'd beaten Ashley by more than three seconds. She gave Storm a long pat.

Ben was waiting outside the ring. "You were on fire!" he exclaimed. "What got into you?"

"Just something Val Grant said," Amy told him.

Ben grinned. "In that case, you should pay her to say something before you go in every class. No one's going to beat that time!"

He was right. Of the twenty horses that followed, none of them beat Storm.

Grinning with delight, Amy rode Storm into the ring to collect the blue ribbon.

Ashley was in second place. As the judge moved down the line, giving out the ribbons, Amy wondered if Ashley would congratulate her, but Ashley stared resolutely ahead. Amy couldn't resist making a comment.

"Magic went well in the ring, Ashley," she said. "You must be really pleased."

"I am. Thanks," Ashley said abruptly.

"I guess your mom doesn't know how you did it, though, does she?" Amy shook her head. "Why don't you say something to her, Ashley? You can't just keep dropping your whip in each class. She *will* notice, you know."

Ashley frowned at her. "It's not that easy."

As Amy saw Ashley's tense face, she remembered Ben's words and felt strangely sorry for the other girl. He was right. It couldn't be easy having Val Grant as your mom. "It's OK," she said more quietly. "I understand."

Ashley stared at her. "What do you mean, you understand?" The judge looked back curiously in their direction. Ashley immediately lowered her voice. "You don't know anything, Amy!" she hissed.

Amy was stung. "I know it can't be easy living and working with a mom like yours."

"You leave my mom out of this!" Ashley whispered furiously.

"Calm down!" Amy said, shrugging. "I was just trying to say I felt sorry for you."

Two bright pink spots of color stained Ashley's cheeks. "You! Feel sorry for me? When my family has Green Briar and all you've got is your run-down little barn with its two muddy training rings and its junkyard horses?" Haughty pride filled her green eyes. "Get real, Amy. Save your sympathy for yourself. I don't need it!"

Just then the steward came back up the line. "Time for your lap of honor," he said cheerfully to Amy. "Off you go."

Amy's cheeks blazed as she pushed Storm into a canter. *That is definitely the last time I try to help Ashley!* she thought. *She and her mom deserve each other!*

Ben was clapping as she rode out. He stopped when he saw her face. "What's up with you?" he said in surprise. "You won! You should be thrilled."

"I am," Amy said with a half smile.

Sensing her tension, Storm threw his head up anxiously. She took a deep breath. "It's OK," she said, patting him. "I'm not angry with you."

Just then Nick Halliwell came over to them.

Amy smiled in surprise, and thoughts of Ashley left her mind.

Nick Halliwell was a show jumper who Amy had first met when she had cured one of his young horses of its fear of trailers. Since then Nick had sent several of his horses to Heartland. They were helping one of his horses — Dylan — at the moment.

"Congratulations, Amy. That was a great round," Nick said. "I was watching in the stands. Your horse can certainly jump," he said, patting Storm's neck.

Amy smiled, glowing at the praise.

"Where did you get him?" Nick asked.

"My dad bought him for me when he was over here on business. He was looking for young sports horses to export to Australia. He found Storm in Florida."

"Well, he's certainly got a good eye. Maybe I should ask your father to keep me in mind," Nick said. "I could use a horse like him." He nodded at Ben. "How's Red going?"

"Good — I hope," Ben replied. "My class is next." He looked at the ring where they'd just finished raising the jumps for the intermediate division. "I'd better walk the course," he said to Amy. "Catch up with you at the trailer."

"Sure," Amy replied.

As Ben left, Nick turned to Amy. "So, how's Dylan?"

"Good," Amy answered. Dylan had come to Heartland because of his poor coordination and lack of balance. She and Ty had put a lot of work into getting him to go through a network of poles on the ground, and his coordination was gradually improving. "He's starting to come together. We just need to work him some more over small jumps. He should be ready to come home soon."

"Good." Nick nodded.

Someone shouted Nick's name. "Look, I've got to go," he said to Amy. "But I'll come and visit soon." He patted Storm. "Take good care of this horse — he's very talented."

He walked off. Feeling delighted at his praise, Amy dismounted and began to walk back to the trailer. She was almost there when she saw her friend Daniel striding across the grass in front of her. She called to him and he stopped.

"Hi," he said with a wave. He brushed his brown hair out of his eyes as she headed over.

"I didn't know you were here today," Amy said.

She had first met Daniel when he was competing on the circuit. At that stage, he had been hoping to get a place as a working pupil at a show-jumping barn, but then he was in a terrible jumping accident and had lost his horse, Amber. After that, he had needed any job he could get and had taken a stable hand position at Green Briar a month ago.

"I've been helping a client who's entered in Amateur Owner," Daniel told her. "How are you? Have you been in the ring yet?"

Amy nodded. "In Junior Jumpers. We won."

Daniel grinned. "How did Ashley do?"

"Second," Amy replied, unable to suppress a triumphant smile.

Daniel raised his eyebrows. "Guess the Grants won't be pleased about that."

Amy grinned. "No. But they should be. Magic looked so much better."

He looked at his watch. "I'm due for a break. Do you have time to chat?"

"Sure," Amy said. "How about we buy a couple of sodas and take them back to the trailer? Then I can untack this guy."

"Sounds great," Daniel replied, giving Storm a pat.

❧

They sat on the ramp of the trailer and drank their Cokes while Storm grazed at the end of his lead rope. "How are things at Green Briar?" Amy asked.

"Not great," Daniel admitted. "At first, I guess I was

just glad to have a job. I needed something to stop me thinking about Amber."

Amy looked at him sympathetically. She knew how hard it was to lose a horse, especially a horse as special as Amber. "But now?"

Daniel hesitated. "I don't know. I thought I wanted a job with no commitment, no emotional involvement, but," he said with a shrug, "to be honest, I'm hating it. I never know which horses I'll be riding. I don't get to develop an understanding with any of them, and I don't think Mrs. Grant wants us to. We're just supposed to go through the paces. Some days all I do is groom."

Amy nodded. "It must be hard."

Daniel shook his head. "It's Mrs. Grant's impatience that gets to me," he went on. "Everything has to be done as quickly as possible. For instance, she bought this horse two weeks ago. He's a looker, and he's won lots in eventing, but he hasn't been ridden for a year since his owner went to college. Mrs. Grant's got him back full time already. Daily one-hour workouts with jumping. She should let his muscles build up gradually, but she wants to sell him before the season ends." He sighed. "I tried to explain that he'll be injury prone in the future if she doesn't take it easy, but she wouldn't listen to me. I find that mentality difficult to deal with."

"So what are you going to do?" Amy asked him curiously.

"Don't know," Daniel replied, shrugging. "Look for another job, I guess."

"Have you thought about looking for a working-pupil position again?" Amy said.

"I'm always looking, but there's nothing available, especially not this time of year." He changed the subject. "So, come on, tell me about you. How's everyone at Heartland?"

Amy filled him in on all the news.

As he listened to her talk, Daniel started to look thoughtful. "You know, you might be able to help me," he said. "There's a young horse at Green Briar — a boarder that's come to be broken in. He's really withdrawn and quiet. His owner told me his stable companion, an old hunter, died a few months ago, and I think he might still be grieving for him. Do you know of anything I can give him that might help?"

"You could try Bach Flower Remedies," Amy answered. "But it's hard to say which one you should use without seeing the horse. There are several that are useful for grief."

"Maybe you could come and take a look at him," Daniel said, "and tell me which one to use."

Amy laughed. "Yeah, Val Grant would really love that! Me on her yard, treating her horses, using alternative methods. I don't think so."

"She's at an all-day show with some clients tomorrow," Daniel said. "You could come then. Please, Amy. This horse seems seriously depressed. He needs help."

Amy hesitated. She was incapable of turning down a horse in need. "Well, I guess I could ask Lou to drop me off for twenty minutes or so," she said reluctantly.

"Thanks!" Daniel said, delighted. He glanced at his watch. "I better move it." He jumped up. "Mrs. Grant's bound to have some work lined up for me. I'll see you tomorrow."

"I'll call you if I can't make it," Amy said. "Otherwise, I'll come about ten."

"See you then," Daniel said.

When it was time for Ben to go in his class, Amy went to watch. "You be good," she told the big chestnut horse as Ben tightened Red's girth after warming up. "Good luck," she said to Ben.

Ben cantered into the ring. Amy watched anxiously, but Red was in top form, and he managed a double clear with a fast time.

"Looks like it's Heartland's day." Ben grinned as he trotted out of the ring, patting Red hard.

He was right. No one else managed to beat his time, and when they drove out of the show ground at lunchtime, there were two blue ribbons displayed on the dashboard, and both Amy and Ben had prize-money checks in their pockets.

Amy looked at the two rosettes. "Why can't every show be like this one?" she said, sighing happily.

"It can," Ben said. "We're the dream team!"

Amy grinned. "The dream team indeed."

Looking out the window, she thought about Storm's round again. It had felt amazing — almost as if they were flying. She thought about her next show in two weeks' time. She couldn't wait to capture that feeling again.

The countryside rolled by, and at last they arrived back at Heartland. As Ben parked the trailer outside the farmhouse, Lou, Amy's older sister, came hurrying to meet them.

Amy jumped out of the pickup and waved the ribbons. "Hey, Lou! Check it out!" she said. "Storm and Red both won their classes and —" She rummaged in her pocket and produced the check she had won. "This is for Heartland."

Lou glanced quickly at the check. "That's good," she said distractedly.

Amy frowned. "What's up?"

Lou ran a hand through her short blond hair. "It's Sundance," she said. "He's sick. I think he has colic."

Chapter Two

"Colic!" Amy exclaimed.

"I called Scott," Lou said, looking worried. "He came over and gave Sundance an antispasmodic injection."

"I'll unload Storm, Amy," Ben said quickly. "You go check on him."

Amy ran up the yard. She felt sick at the thought of Sundance being in pain — and her not being there to comfort him.

She reached the barn. Ty was standing in Sundance's stall. The buckskin pony was moving from one leg to the other restlessly. Seeing Amy, he lifted his head and whickered.

"How is he?" Amy asked, going into the stall.

"A little better," Ty replied. "The injection seems to be kicking in."

Sundance pushed his nose into Amy's chest. Amy rubbed his golden ears, and he sighed deeply, as if relieved that she was finally with him.

"How did it happen?" she asked Ty.

"There doesn't seem to be any obvious reason," Ty replied. "About half an hour after you'd gone, I noticed that he was looking restless. The next time I came by, he was rubbing his belly up against the stall. Then he sort of collapsed and tried to roll. I got him back up on his feet and then called Scott. We couldn't find anything that might have triggered it. Scott thinks it's just one of those things. Maybe it has to do with the heat or his lack of work since he's been recuperating." He put an arm around her shoulders.

Amy felt a wave of guilt as the pony nuzzled her. "I should have been here," she said.

"You were only gone for half a day," Ty said reasonably. "It could just as easily have happened when you were at school or out shopping or something."

Amy gave him a funny look — when did she ever have time to go shopping? She kept stroking Sundance and didn't say anything.

Ty shook his head. "Come on. Don't beat yourself up over it. Everything's fine now."

Logically, she knew Ty was right, but somehow she felt worse knowing that she had been at a show, enjoying herself.

"Look, why don't you stay here with him for a while,"
Ty said. "I'll get back to work. With this happening, I'm
way behind. Lou and your grandpa have been great,
though. They did all the mucking out, but we've still got
to exercise the horses. If you stay with Sundance, I can
get started."

Amy nodded. "Thanks, Ty."

"No problem," he said.

Amy kissed Sundance's forehead and started to move
her fingers in small circles on his neck. It was a form of
therapy called T-touch that Amy had learned from her
mother. As she gently pushed his skin over his muscles, she
breathed deeply and shut her eyes. If only she hadn't gone
to the show. *Still,* she told herself as her fingers worked
over Sundance's neck, *I'm here now. That's all that matters.*

Half an hour later, Sundance's head hung low and his
eyes were closed. He looked relaxed and calm, and Amy
crept from the stall. He needed his rest.

She made her way down the yard. Storm was looking
over his half door. Ben had taken his traveling boots off
and brushed him over, but he still had his braids in. He
nuzzled Amy in a puzzled sort of way. Amy understood.
Normally, when they came home from a show, she spent
time brushing him, unbraiding him, and massaging his
legs. He must have been wondering where she was.

Just then, Lou came out of the tack room. She was carrying some scissors and a small stool. "There you are. I was just going to unbraid him for you."

Amy smiled gratefully. "Thanks, Lou." She reached for the scissors and stool. "I can do it. Sundance is resting now."

"I don't mind if you want to get started riding the other horses," Lou said. "I know there's still a lot to do today."

Amy knew she should take Lou's offer to help, but she didn't want to just go off and leave Storm. He'd been so good at the show. She hesitated, feeling torn.

"I really don't mind," Lou insisted.

"OK, thanks, Lou," Amy said, forcing a smile. "I'll go find Ty and see what I can do."

Ty was riding Dylan around the ring on a loose rein. Seeing Amy walking up to the gate, he rode Dylan over. "How's the patient?"

"Resting," Amy said. "Who do you want me to work?"

"Well, I'm just about done with Dylan, and Ben's coming in here next to school Major. You could start work with Willow if you think she's ready."

Amy looked at the next-door pasture where Willow, a bright bay pony of about fourteen hands, was grazing.

Willow had been traumatized by a bad experience with an old-fashioned horse breaker. The breaker had been the pony's first exposure to people. He had taken the young pony straight off the fields, tied her to a post, and beaten her in an attempt to crush her spirit. Willow was a nervous pony to start with, and now she was completely terrified of people. Her new owners had kind hearts but little experience with horses, so they had sent Willow to Heartland in hopes that Amy and Ty could help the pony regain her confidence.

Amy walked over to Willow's paddock. She didn't really have a plan of what to do, but sometimes that was the best way of working with a difficult horse. Amy knew that going in with a set plan could be an impediment — it could keep her from listening to what the horse really needed.

As Amy opened the gate, Willow trotted to the far side of the field. Amy watched her for a moment and then walked into the center of the pasture. She had no rope and she made no sudden movements, but just the very sight of her approaching made Willow throw her head up in fear. With a snort, the pony took off around the pasture, her head angled to the outside of the field.

Shoulders rounded, head down, Amy stood very still. At first, Willow cantered blindly, but as the minutes passed, she began to slow down. She still didn't dare to glance in Amy's direction, but after a few more laps she slowed to a halt. She stood for a moment and then wheeled around and set off in the opposite direction.

Amy didn't move. Willow kept on cantering, but after

a few more laps, it was clear she was starting to tire. Dark patches of sweat were appearing on her back, and she was breathing quickly. She slowed to a trot. As soon as she did so, Amy had an idea. She took a few steps backward. She wanted Willow to realize that she wasn't trying to hurt her, that the pony could slow down and Amy wouldn't try to catch her. Willow trotted another lap before slowing to a walk. Amy quickly stepped back another few steps. As if realizing what was going on, Willow halted and turned to look at her for the first time.

To reward the pony, Amy backed slowly out of the ring.

Ben was riding Major in the schooling ring. Seeing Amy leave Willow's field, he rode over. "Doesn't she want to join up with you?" he asked.

Join up was a technique they used a lot at Heartland. It was a way of communicating with the horse and gaining its trust, but Amy hadn't been trying to do that with Willow. "I wasn't trying to get her to join up with me," she told Ben. "All I wanted was for her to look at me."

She saw him frown in confusion.

"When you join up with a horse you have to use aggressive body language to chase the horse away from you," Amy explained. "Willow's much too frightened to be able to cope with someone doing that just now. If I'd tried it, she would have ended up even more scared."

Ben shook his head. "You know, I could work here for ten years and I still wouldn't be able to figure the needs of each individual horse like you can," he said. "How do you do it?"

Amy shrugged. "It just comes to me." She paused, uncertain whether to say more, but Ben looked genuinely interested so she decided to elaborate. "I didn't always know what to do." She hesitated. "After Mom died, I felt really helpless. Whenever I worked with a horse I just kept trying to figure out what she would have done. But then I gradually started to trust my own instincts. Now I just seem to know what's needed — not all the time, of course," she qualified. "But more than I used to."

"You and Ty are something else," Ben said. "I'll never have your instincts."

"Well, you have other talents," Amy told him, knowing it was useless to pretend otherwise. "You can stay on anything. Major would have had me off five times already if I'd been working with him. You haven't fallen off once."

Ben grinned. "Superglue on the saddle. You should try it."

They exchanged smiles. Amy patted Major. "Well, I'd better get moving," she said. "See you soon."

❧

The rest of the day raced by. Amy worked with Willow twice more, each time simply standing in the middle of the field and waiting until the pony felt brave enough to look at her, and then rewarding her bravery by backing away and leaving. On the third time it only took the little bay a few minutes of cantering around before she stopped and looked at Amy. She still showed no signs of coming anywhere near her, but there seemed to be a new curiosity in her eyes, as if she was starting to think about what Amy was doing rather than just blindly running away. Amy was satisfied. The progress Willow was making might be slow, but at least it was progress.

By the time the last hay net had been put into the last stall at six o'clock, Amy was wiped out from her long day. It seemed a long time since she had gotten up that morning. She waved good-bye to Ty and Ben and then went wearily to Storm's stall. He pushed her affectionately with his nose. Amy sighed. She knew she should spend some time with him.

"I'm sorry, Storm," she told him, stroking his nose. "But I'm beat."

He nuzzled her, not understanding. Amy rested her forehead against his face, feeling torn. She was just so tired. Her stomach growled ravenously.

"Tomorrow," she told him and, giving him a last kiss, she walked to the house.

Chapter Three

"I'll come back to pick you up in half an hour," Lou said when she dropped Amy off in the parking lot at Green Briar the next morning.

Amy nodded. "Thanks." Half expecting someone to stop her and demand to know what she, Amy Fleming, was doing at Green Briar Stable, she walked hesitantly toward the barns. All three training rings had horses working in them, and in the jumping ring, she could see a beautiful steel-gray Trakehner completing a course of four-foot fences. The rider drew him to a halt and gave him a brusque single pat. Then, swinging her leg over the saddle, she dismounted and handed the reins to a stable hand in one swift motion. "Here. I'm done," she said, and, without so much as a glance back at the horse, she strode from the ring.

"Amy!"

Amy looked around and saw Daniel hurrying toward her.

"Thanks for coming," he said. "Come and meet Midnight, the horse I told you about. He's in one of the back barns."

Amy followed him across the yard. It was immaculate. Hardly a strand of straw littered the ground, and all the brooms and shovels were hanging on a wall. Daniel walked into a barn and stopped at the door of the second stall. A black colt with a white blaze was standing quietly in one corner, his head down, his muzzle almost resting on his straw bed.

"That's all he does," Daniel said. "He just stands there like that."

Amy went into the stall and Daniel followed. The colt didn't even look up. "You said his stable companion died?" she said.

"Yes," Daniel replied. "It was the owner's old hunter. Midnight had been stalled next to him ever since he was weaned."

Amy stroked the colt's black coat. "What happens when you turn him out?"

"He grazes, but he's very withdrawn," Daniel said.

"And what about feeding?" Amy asked, her eyes not leaving the subdued colt.

"He eats OK," Daniel replied. "He likes his food."

Amy thought for a moment. "Give him the honeysuckle Bach Flower Remedy," she said at last. "It's the best remedy for loss. If Midnight was so uninterested in life that he wouldn't eat, wild rose or olive might work better, but I think honeysuckle is the one you need. Add ten drops to his water each day, and maybe give him ten drops of walnut as well — it will help him adjust to the change in his surroundings."

"Thanks," Daniel said. "I hate seeing him so low."

Amy patted the colt. "You'll get better soon, Midnight. You're lucky Daniel's here."

They left the stall. "So how are you feeling about yesterday?" Daniel asked. "Have you come back down to earth yet?" He responded to her blank expression. "Amy, the show?" he said emphatically. "Winning Junior Jumper."

Realization dawned on Amy's face. "Oh, that."

Daniel shook his head. "Amy! Most people wouldn't be able to think of anything else for at least a week!"

"I know, and I'm thrilled," she said. "It's just that there's a lot going on at Heartland right now." She tried to explain. "I never seem to have time for everything. There are so many horses that need our help at the moment."

"It must be tough," Daniel said sympathetically.

Amy nodded. Although she kept trying to convince herself she could keep up with everything, it was getting harder to go to shows in addition to doing all her work at Heartland. The last few days had proven that, with Sundance getting colic while she was at the show. She sighed. She always seemed to feel guilty about something — Sundance, Storm, Lou helping in the yard, Ty being overworked.

They walked back out to the yard. A handsome dark bay horse of about sixteen hands was in the cross ties farther down the aisle. A stable hand was standing beside his shoulder. Another stood by his haunches, with a broom raised.

Amy frowned. "What's going on?" she asked Daniel.

"Lately, Duke's been irritable whenever anyone has tried to pick his hooves," Daniel replied. "I told you about him. He's the horse that's won quite a lot but has been out to pasture the last year."

"Oh, yeah," Amy said, remembering. "The one Val's got back to a full work schedule already."

Daniel nodded. "He was great until a few days ago, but when the farrier came he just freaked. Ever since then, he won't let anyone touch his feet."

"Maybe the farrier hammered a nail too close to the sensitive part of his hoof," Amy suggested.

"He didn't get as far as actually putting shoes on," Daniel replied. "Duke revolted as soon as he tried to put his hoof on the stand. Val thinks he's just being stubborn, but he doesn't strike me as that kind of horse."

Amy watched as the stable hand near Duke's shoulder reached down to pick up the horse's hoof. The second he touched Duke's leg, the horse flung himself backward.

"Stop that!" the stable hand behind him shouted, smacking him with the broom.

Amy flinched. She saw the fear in the horse's eyes. "He's scared," she said quickly to Daniel.

The first stable hand was reaching for Duke's leg again. This time the horse's ears went back even before the stable hand had touched him. He half reared, pulling at the chains attached to his halter, but the broom smacked into him once again. Duke threw his head, his eyes flashing white. "Stand still!" the stable hand shouted, hitting him again.

"Daniel! Please stop them!" Amy said urgently.

Daniel stepped forward. "Hey, you guys." The stable hands looked around. "Why don't you give Duke a break? He's all worked up. Maybe you should let him cool off a while."

"We're just doing what Mrs. Grant told us to do — teach him a lesson." He waved the broom behind Duke, and the horse lunged forward until the cross-tie chains halted him, snapping his head back.

Amy couldn't restrain herself any longer. "But can't you see he's frightened? Look at him! You're not teaching him anything except to not trust you."

The stable hand looked at Daniel. "Who's your girl-friend?"

Before Amy could tell him, Daniel stepped forward. "She's just a friend," he said, putting a warning hand on her arm. Immediately, she realized that he didn't want them to know who she was or that she was from Heart-land. "Look, guys. Leave Duke. He's a good horse. He doesn't deserve this. I'll talk to Mrs. Grant about him."

To Amy's relief, the stable hand shrugged and put the broom down. "Well, if that's what you want. You can deal with her then."

Daniel pulled Amy's arm. "Come on."

"Idiots," Amy muttered under her breath as she walked away.

"They're only doing what they were told," Daniel said. "Mrs. Grant believes that all horses should be forced to learn respect."

Amy shook her head. "I don't know how you can stand to work here."

Daniel shrugged. "It's a job. I get paid."

Amy looked at him. "You don't mean that."

For a moment, Daniel didn't reply, and then he sighed. "No, I don't," he admitted. "I hate it, but I do need the work."

"So get another job," Amy told him.

"If only," Daniel said. "I don't have a reference from my last job because I left so suddenly, and the Grants aren't likely to give me one if I leave here so soon. No decent stables will look at me without references."

Amy saw the despondency on his face. "Something will come up," she said hopefully. "I'm sure it will." She glanced at her watch. "I'd better go. Lou will be here any minute."

As she spoke, Ashley came around the corner. She was wearing cream breeches and a DKNY T-shirt. "Amy!" the name burst from her in surprise. "What are you doing here?"

"I —" Amy didn't know what to say.

"She just stopped by to say hi to me," Daniel said quickly.

Ashley turned on him, her eyes narrowing. "Shouldn't you be working?"

"I'm on a break," he replied curtly.

"Well, when you're off it, which I'm sure is quite soon, I'd like Magic saddled up," Ashley ordered.

"Ever heard of the word *please*, Ashley?" Amy questioned, raising her eyebrows.

Ashley swung around to look at her. "Listen, it's clear that I don't like you and you don't like me, Amy," she snapped, "so why don't you just stay away from my family's stable?"

"With pleasure," Amy retorted. She glanced at Daniel. "I'll call you."

"OK, see you," he replied.

Amy marched away. To her relief, Lou was just pulling into the parking lot. Amy opened the door and jumped in. "Get me out of here fast," she said desperately.

Lou glanced at the yard and grinned. "Let me guess — you saw Ashley Grant?"

"Got it in one," Amy replied.

When Amy got back to Heartland, she helped Ben and Ty finish the stalls, then she went to Willow's pasture. She worked the pony just as she had done the day before, letting her run the perimeter and then rewarding her for stopping.

The fifth time she entered the paddock, Willow merely trotted around several times before halting. She looked at Amy and then lowered her head. There was a new softness in her expression, a certain curiosity. Amy took a small step backward and paused. Willow hesitated and then took one tentative step toward her.

"Good girl," Amy whispered. She left the paddock, her spirits high.

She went to Storm's stall. He had been out in the field, and she was relieved to see that there wasn't any swelling in his legs from his hard work the day before. "I'll give you a good brushing," she said, "and then I'll massage your tendons with black pepper and eucalyptus oils so you won't be stiff tomorrow."

She gathered her grooming kit and the diluted oils and set to work. Storm seemed to love the attention. As she massaged the warming oil into his legs, he snorted happily. He was such an affectionate horse it made her feel doubly bad when she was too busy to spend time with him.

Straightening up after doing his two front legs, Amy rested her head against his warm neck and breathed in his sweet smell. "I love you, boy," she told him.

"Amy!"

She went to the door. Ty was looking for her. "Can you help me with Dylan?"

Amy's heart sank. She hadn't finished Storm yet. But what could she do? "OK," she called back resignedly.

She patted the gray gelding. "I'll be back soon," she promised.

But after she'd helped with Dylan, Ty reminded her that they had to move some more hay from the main barn to the small feed room and then they had to sweep up. In the end, it was almost an hour before she got back to Storm's stall.

Feeling the tension mounting inside her at the thought of everything she had to do, she unbolted Storm's door. "Hi, Storm. I'm back."

He nuzzled her in greeting.

She had just picked up the bottle of oil when she heard Ben calling her name. She looked over the door.

"Can you give me a hand bringing some of the horses in so Jack can work on the gate?" he asked.

No, Amy felt like shouting, but she knew she couldn't. Taking a deep breath, she put down the oil and left Storm's stall. "Fine," she said.

Ben must have heard the tension in her voice. "What's up?" he asked in surprise.

"Nothing," she replied abruptly. "Do you have the leads?"

Storm put his head over the door and whinnied in surprise as she walked away. Amy felt awful. *Still*, she told herself, *all I've got to do is help bring the ponies in and then I can get back to him*. "I'll get Solly," she told Ben, taking a lead rope from him.

Ben nodded and haltered Jigsaw and Jasmine.

Solitaire, a headstrong yearling who was at Heartland to learn some stable etiquette, was at the other side of the field watching curiously as Grandpa fixed a bar in the fence that had come loose.

Please be good, Amy thought.

As soon as the chestnut foal saw the other two ponies being led out of the field, she came trotting over to the gate.

"Here, Solly," Amy called.

To her relief, Solitaire walked straight up to her.

"Good girl," Amy praised as she buckled up her halter. She opened the gate, and the foal immediately barged forward, trying to catch up with Jigsaw and Jasmine.

"No!" Amy said, stopping her. "You mustn't pull!"

Turning the foal in a circle, she led her back into the field and started to walk down the yard again. Solitaire walked three paces and then raced forward after the ponies.

"Solly! Stop that!" Amy said.

Feeling her frustration mounting, she turned Solitaire back to the gate. "You are not going down to the barn if you pull like that," she told her. "Just walk nicely!"

The foal looked after Jigsaw and Jasmine and whinnied loudly. It was clear she wanted to be with them.

"Come on," Amy pleaded with her. "I don't have time for this." She clicked her tongue. Solitaire walked beside her for ten paces. Amy was just breathing a sigh of relief when, suddenly, the little foal barged forward, the impact from her shoulder throwing Amy off balance.

"Solitaire!" Amy exclaimed, pulling sharply on the lead. "Stop it!" Solitaire half reared. As she came down, one of her front hooves landed squarely on Amy's foot.

"Ow!" Amy cried. Pain and anger blinded her, and her hand flew up. "You stupid —"

She stopped on the very point of smacking Solitaire's

neck. The world seemed to stand very still for a moment, and then slowly she lowered her arm. She breathed out shakily. What was she thinking? She'd almost hit her! Amy gave the foal a nudge with her hip to get her to move off her foot. She breathed slowly, composing herself.

"Amy?"

She swung around to see Grandpa hurrying across the field toward her, a look of concern on his face. "What's going on?"

Chapter Four

Amy stared at her grandfather with horrified eyes, then she turned back to Solitaire. Completely oblivious to the situation, the chestnut foal pulled impatiently in the direction of the barn.

"Amy," Grandpa said when he reached them. "What's the matter?"

"I — I almost hit her," Amy said, her face pale with shock.

"Oh, Amy. That's not like you. You're just tired — you overreacted," Grandpa said, putting a comforting hand on her arm. "Here. Take a few moments out. I'll take Solitaire."

Amy felt embarrassed by his concern and understanding. She started to hand him the lead rope, but then she stopped. "No. I have to do this," she said. Taking a deep breath, she touched the foal's neck. "Come on, Solly," she said, forcing her voice to sound calm and controlled. "Back to the gate."

She led the foal back up the path. Inside she was still reeling from the shock of what she had almost done, but she was determined to get Solitaire to lead without losing her temper.

It took three more attempts but, finally, Solly seemed to get the message that lunging and pulling would only result in her being taken back to the gate. On the fourth time, she walked quietly beside Amy all the way to the barn. Amy took her halter off as she opened the stall door.

"See, it wasn't so difficult after all," she said, patting the horse. She spoke cheerfully, but inside she was very aware of Grandpa watching her, his forehead furrowed.

"Amy," he said as she tried to hurry past him with the halter. "Are you OK?"

Amy stopped. "I think so."

"Let's go to the house," Grandpa said quietly. "We should talk. I'm worried about you."

Her heart thudding, Amy followed him across the lawn.

Grandpa went into the kitchen. Amy hovered by the doorway.

"What's going on, Amy?" Grandpa asked softly. "I've never known you to lose your temper with a horse."

Amy rubbed her forehead with one hand. "I was just feeling stressed, I guess."

Grandpa sighed. "You have been working very long hours."

"I'm doing OK," Amy said quickly.

"Are you?" Grandpa fixed her with his blue eyes. He put a hand on her shoulder. "I get this feeling that you're not very happy at the moment." He shook his head. "You have too much going on. You can't enjoy any of it. Look, how about you ease up on your workload with the horses? We could get some temporary help."

Amy stared at him in shock. Cut back on working with the horses! "No," she said quickly. "I couldn't do that."

"Well, maybe you should think again about competing Storm," Grandpa suggested. "Maybe you don't have time for that as well as everything else."

"But I love the shows," Amy protested. She shook her head. "No. I'll be fine, Grandpa. Really I will. I'm just adjusting to the new schedule."

He looked doubtful.

Just then the kitchen door opened, and Lou came in from the office. She took in the tension on Amy's face. "What's wrong?"

"Amy and I are trying to work out a way to make her life less hectic so she can enjoy the summer a little," Grandpa replied.

Lou frowned in concern. "You *have* been working really hard lately," she said to Amy. "Maybe I could help more," she offered. "Now that I've got the advertising all set up I have more time on my hands. I could groom Storm for you each day and clean his tack before shows if it would help." She shot Amy a quick smile. "Just don't ask me to ride him."

Amy half smiled. A few weeks back, Lou had tried to ride Storm, but it had been a disaster. Because she had just started riding again after thirteen years out of the saddle, Lou's leg and hand signals had been far too abrupt for a sensitive, highly schooled horse like Storm.

"I could do other things, too," Lou continued. "I don't know enough to work the difficult horses, but I could ride some of the quieter ponies, like Jasmine and Jigsaw, that only need light exercise on the trails. Just let me know what to do."

"Thanks, Lou," Amy said.

"I'd be happy to do your share of the stalls on show days," Grandpa said.

"I'd appreciate that," Amy said.

He smiled. "We're both here for you, Amy. We both want to help you any way we can."

"Thanks," Amy said. But she knew there wasn't any more they could do. It was working with the problem horses that took up most of her time, and that was one job that she couldn't hand over to anyone else even if she wanted to. She stood up. "I'd better get going," she said. "I'll see you both later."

They nodded, and she hurried out of the kitchen.

❧

Over the next few days, Lou started grooming Storm and cleaning his tack. It saved Amy some time, but she found she really missed spending time in his stall with him. Several times Amy caught herself thinking back over Grandpa's words and wondering whether she really could keep on going as she was. It was hard enough now, but what would happen when she went back to school in a few weeks time? She knew she would never cut back on working with the horses. So what was she going to do? *Nothing,* she decided, pushing her concerns to the back of her mind. *I'll just carry on as I have been. I'll cope.*

❧

On Thursday morning, Daniel called Amy. "Hi," he said. "I thought I'd give you an update on Midnight."

"How is he?" Amy asked, remembering the black colt.

"Doing well," Daniel replied. "I added the remedies to his water on Monday, and he's been like a different horse. He's stopped standing in the corner all the time, and he's taking more of an interest in things."

"That's great," Amy said, feeling pleased that she'd been able to help.

"How have you been?" Daniel asked her.

"Busy," Amy answered. "How about you? Seen any new job postings yet?"

"No," Daniel answered. "And Mrs. Grant's driving me crazy. Do you remember Duke? The horse that wouldn't let anyone pick his feet?"

As if she could forget. "Yes, I remember him," Amy answered.

"Well, now she has handlers standing behind him with a crop, hitting him every time he moves back. The horse is totally freaked out. He used to be really approachable in his stall, but now you can't get near him. He constantly has his ears back, and he's always threatening to bite or kick."

An image of the handsome bay gelding came into Amy's mind. He'd had such a wise face; it was awful to think of him becoming so confused and scared that he had taken to kicking. "Can't you do anything?" But even as she spoke she knew what the answer would be. Val Grant ruled Green Briar with an iron fist, and she wouldn't stand for any of her lowly stable hands telling her what she should or shouldn't be doing.

"Like what?" Daniel said. "I got into enough trouble after stopping Jed and Kevin that time you visited. Mrs.

Grant has put me on a formal warning. If I step out of line again, I lose my job." He sighed in frustration. "I just wish she could see that what she's doing is going to ruin Duke."

Amy heard the unhappiness in his voice. "Look, why don't you come and visit us here?" she suggested. "When's your next day off?"

"Sunday," Daniel replied.

"Well, come over," Amy said. "You haven't seen Ty or Grandpa or Lou for ages. I'm sure they'd really like to catch up with you."

"All right," Daniel said, sounding more cheerful. "I'd love to visit. I'll come by about ten if that's OK."

"Great," Amy said. "Do you want to stay for brunch as well?"

"I'd love to," Daniel said. "Thanks. See you Sunday."

After Amy replaced the receiver, she sat down at the table. She couldn't stop thinking about Duke. She hated the thought of him becoming aggressive. She chewed on a fingernail. If only there were something she could do. But Val Grant was hardly likely to listen to her, and if Daniel said anything he'd get fired, and then he wouldn't have a job or anywhere to live.

Amy sighed and stood up. Well, there were horses outside that she *could* help. She'd better go and get started with them.

ℜ

Willow was grazing in the field. As Amy opened the gate, the pony looked up sharply but didn't run away, and Amy felt a glow of satisfaction. Every moment she was spending with Willow was paying off.

She walked to the center of the field. Willow moved away, but instead of cantering blindly around the pasture, too scared to even look in Amy's direction, now she simply trotted away. Her eyes darted toward Amy every few paces. Amy stood still. After two laps, Willow slowed to a halt.

Amy stepped backward. Willow took a step toward her. To reward the pony for her bravery, Amy walked back another pace. Willow stared at her intently. Acting on instinct, Amy turned away and crouched down near the ground. There was a long pause, and then she heard Willow starting to walk toward her across the paddock.

Amy's heart beat with anticipation, but she forced herself to stay still. This was the first time Willow had taken more than just a step or two toward her. She could hear Willow's hooves on the grass. The pony was close now, almost close enough to touch. Amy felt the air move as Willow reached down, and then her muzzle brushed against Amy's shoulders.

Amy counted to three and then, moving very slowly, she turned. Willow stared down at her, her dark eyes wide and watchful. Reaching up, Amy touched Willow's neck.

The pony tensed for a moment, and then a long sigh left her. Not daring to stand up in case she frightened her, Amy gently rubbed her neck.

Willow lowered her head and started grazing by Amy's feet. Amy waited for five minutes until the pony had moved a couple of feet away and then slowly straightened up. Willow raised her head anxiously.

"It's OK," Amy whispered, not wanting to push too much in one day. "I'm going now." She started to back toward the gate. Willow hesitated and then came after her. Amy's heart leaped. Willow was choosing to be with her. She wanted to join up.

Reaching the gate, Amy stopped and stroked the pony's shoulder. Willow's skin twitched, but she stood quietly, her eyes on Amy's face, full of trust. Amy smiled in delight. They had reached an understanding — they would be friends.

Over the next two days, Amy spent as much time with Willow as she could. With each session, Willow's confidence seemed to grow. By Saturday night, Amy could pat her all over.

"You are doing really well, Willow," Amy praised as she led the pony around the paddock.

Willow suddenly tensed and looked in the direction of the gate. Amy glanced around. Ty was there. "It's OK," Amy said softly. "Ty won't hurt you."

Willow was still very nervous around people other than Amy. She stared anxiously in Ty's direction, her muscles tensed. To show that she was listening to her and that she understood her fear, Amy unbuckled the halter and set the pony free. "See?" she said. "I won't make you go near Ty if you don't want to."

She patted Willow, then walked over to the gate.

"How is she?" Ty asked.

"Good," Amy replied. She glanced around. Willow was following her. The pony stopped about nine feet away from the gate, but the fact that she had come so close to Ty was a huge improvement. "She's getting braver every day."

"I'm headed home now," Ty said. "Everything's done in the barns. Are you almost finished?"

"Not yet. I'm going to ride Storm," Amy said, leaving the paddock and starting to walk to his truck with him.

Ty looked at her ruefully. "I guess it's no use asking if you want to go out and catch a movie, then?"

Amy was torn. She really wanted to say yes, but if she went to a movie then she wouldn't have time to ride Storm, and she had a big show coming up in just a week's time — her first time ever competing in the High Junior Jumper Class.

"Hey, don't stress about it," Ty said, seeming to see her confusion. "It's OK, I realize the horses come first. You know I understand that."

He spoke sympathetically, but Amy still felt bad. They were supposed to be dating, but they never went anywhere together. Still, when did she have the time?

"See you," Ty said and, putting his hands on her shoulders, he kissed her.

Amy shut her eyes and then leaned her head on his shoulder.

"See you," she whispered as they parted.

"Tomorrow," Ty said, completing her sentence with a smile.

❧

That night a strong wind blew up, and when Amy went outside to feed the horses the following morning, there was loose straw from the muck heap blowing all over the yard.

"Oh, great," Amy muttered, looking around at the mess. Cleaning it up was going to take time.

Ignoring the whinnies of the horses in the front stable block eager for their breakfast, she hurried to check on the pastures. During the summer months, most of the ponies at Heartland lived outside day and night, and Amy was worried that the wind might have damaged some of the fences or brought down a tree.

To her relief, all seemed calm in the pastures. The fences seemed to still be intact, if a little battered, and Jigsaw, Ivy, Solitaire, Jasmine, Sugarfoot, and Blackjack were all grazing happily, their manes and tails blowing in the wind.

Willow was the only pony not grazing. She was pacing around, her head held high, her eyes tense and worried. Amy climbed over the gate. The little bay gave a relieved whicker and trotted over. "It's OK, girl," Amy told her as the pony stopped and nudged her anxiously with her nose. The wind often made even calm horses nervous, and Willow was looking wound up.

Amy gently smoothed the pony's forelock. "There's nothing to get worked up about," she told her. "It's just the wind." Gradually, Willow relaxed.

"I'm going to have to go and feed," Amy said after ten minutes. "But you'll be all right. Look at the other ponies. They're not worried."

Willow snorted and, giving her a last pat, Amy left the field.

❧

By the time Daniel arrived at ten o'clock, the wind had dropped slightly and Willow seemed more settled. After saying hi to everyone, Daniel went with Amy to Storm's stall. "How's he going?" he asked her.

"Really well," Amy said, stroking the gelding's neck.

"He sure looks happy," Daniel said. Lou had already groomed Storm that morning, and the dark gray dapples on his snowy-white coat gleamed. Amy agreed that Storm looked content, and she laughed as she watched Daniel tickle the horse's muzzle.

"Do you want to ride him?" Amy offered.

"May I?" Daniel said eagerly. "Will he be OK in the wind?"

Amy nodded. "He's a real honey. Nothing ever seems to upset him."

She tacked Storm up and led him to the training ring. Just as Amy had predicted, Storm ignored the wind and did everything she asked, walking, trotting, and cantering almost intuitively.

When Storm was warmed up, she rode him over to the gate. Dismounting, she handed the reins to Daniel. "OK," she said. "Now you have a turn."

Daniel fastened his hard hat and mounted. At first he simply walked and trotted Storm on a loose rein while they got used to each other, but then he asked the gelding to work a little harder, getting Storm to collect and work through transitions and lateral work.

Amy watched, fascinated. She'd never really seen Storm being ridden before. Daniel rode lightly, like she did, and Storm went very well. They hopped over the short verticals in the center of the ring without breaking stride.

"I'll raise the fences for you," she called after ten minutes.

Jogging into the center of the ring, she set the bar at just over three feet.

Daniel cantered Storm around, and they soared over it.

"Shall I raise it?" Amy called.

"Sure," Daniel said, patting Storm.

Amy raised the jump to three feet six. When Storm cleared that, she raised it again to just over four feet. Once again, he jumped it perfectly, powering upward from his hocks and clearing it with room to spare.

Daniel rode over to Amy, his eyes shining. "Incredible!" he said. "It's like he could jump anything."

Amy nodded, delighted to have someone else share her appreciation of her horse. "No doubt, he's fantastic," she enthused.

Daniel looked at the fence. "Do you want to put it higher?"

"Sure," Amy said. As she raised the pole, she glanced at Daniel. He was circling Storm in a trot, his lips moving as he spoke quietly to the gelding. He turned Storm toward the fence. Storm's ears pricked. He found his stride perfectly, rising through the air and clearing the fence with inches to spare.

Patting him hard, Daniel slowed him to a trot. "You are so lucky," he said, riding up to Amy, his eyes glowing. "This horse is loaded with talent."

"I know," Amy said with a smile.

Just then Storm flinched as an empty plastic feed sack blew up the yard and was caught between the links of the gate. Storm's ears pricked, and he started to back away from the rustling.

"It's OK, boy," Amy told him quickly and, feeling her hand on his neck, he relaxed.

"Amy!" Daniel said quickly. "There's something wrong with the pony in the far field!"

Already hearing the sound of hooves, Amy turned around. Willow was galloping around her pasture, her ears pinned back, her stride furious and reckless.

"It's the feed sack!" Amy gasped. She ran across the ring, chasing after the sack. The sound of the coarse plastic crackling and rustling was clearly upsetting Willow. Amy could only guess that it somehow reminded her of her experience with the horse breaker. Amy grabbed the sack and crumpled it into a ball, but Willow was too terrified to notice that the noise had stopped. Head high, eyes full of panic, she was galloping straight toward the fence.

Chapter Five

"No!" Amy whispered in horror as Willow approached the fence. What would she do? Would she try to jump? She'd never clear it. The pony's muscles tensed, but the fence was high and at the last minute she balked. Her hooves slipped on the short grass, and she fell.

"Ty!" Amy shouted in alarm. She scrambled over the training ring fence. "Ty! Ben! Come quick!"

Dumping the crumpled sack into a nearby bucket, she raced into Willow's pasture. The pony was already struggling to her feet, dust and loose strands of grass falling from her sides.

"Hush, girl," Amy soothed, slowing to a walk so as not to risk alarming her. To her relief she saw that Willow seemed to be bearing weight on all her legs. *Please don't be badly injured*, she prayed.

Willow whickered as she saw her. Reaching her, Amy put her hand on the pony's warm neck. "There, now," she said. "Everything's going to be OK."

Willow pushed her head against Amy's chest and breathed out heavily as if to say, *I know I'm safe now. You're here.*

Amy's eyes raked the pony's body for injuries. There were a few minor cuts, but that seemed to be all. Hearing voices at the gate, she glanced around. Ty and Ben had heard her shouts and had come running across the lawn. Daniel seemed to be explaining to them what had happened.

The next minute, Amy saw Ty hurrying across the field.

Hearing his footsteps, Willow threw her head up nervously. Ty stopped. "Is she OK?" he called anxiously.

"I think so," Amy replied, starting to check the pony over more closely.

"Daniel said she just took off around the field," Ty said.

"A feed sack blew against the gate," Amy explained. "She panicked at the sound — it must have reminded her of the horse breaker. It was a harsh cracking sound, like a whip." She stroked the filly's face. "I'd better stay with her. Can you ask Daniel to put Storm away for me?"

"Sure," Ty said. "Call me if you need me."

✌

Twenty minutes later, Willow had calmed down enough for Amy to lead her down to a stall. To her relief, the young pony seemed to have nothing more wrong with her than a few bumps and bruises.

Ty was filling a water bucket in the yard. "How is she?"

"Quieter," Amy replied. "She doesn't seem to have hurt herself, but I think I'll add some Rescue Remedy to her water to help her get over the shock. Where's Daniel?"

"With Storm," Ty said.

Amy went to find them. Daniel had unsaddled Storm and was standing with the gelding, his fingers moving over Storm's face in the same light T-touch circles that Amy always used.

They both looked so peaceful. "Hey there," Amy whispered.

Daniel looked up and smiled.

Amy let herself into the stall. "Thanks for bringing him in for me."

"No problem. How's the pony?"

"Calm now," Amy said. She looked at Storm's contented expression. "He seems to be enjoying himself."

"He's a special horse," Daniel said warmly.

"A special horse that doesn't get enough attention, do you, boy?" Amy said, stroking Storm's shoulder.

"It must be tough, trying to compete him and do everything here," Daniel said.

"It is," Amy said. She looked at Storm. "Lou's been grooming him for me and cleaning his tack, but it's still difficult to get time to ride him, let alone take him to shows. I always have more than enough to do with the other horses, and he usually comes last."

"Look, if I can help at all, just let me know," Daniel said. "If you need a hand exercising him, I could come by after work."

Amy shook her head. "Thanks, but it wouldn't work. It's weird enough having Lou grooming him for me. If you were exercising him as well, then I'd never spend any time with him. I'd just be getting on him at shows, and that's not right. I want to really work with him, so we can be a team."

"I understand," Daniel said. "But let the offer stand. Just in case."

"Thanks," Amy said.

"Amy, are you there?"

Hearing Lou's voice, Amy looked out over the door.

"Nick Halliwell's on the phone," Lou called from the house. "He wants to stop by and see Dylan in about half an hour. Can I tell him that's OK?"

"Sure," Amy called. She turned back to Daniel with a frantic expression. "I'd better go groom him before Nick gets here."

"I'll give you a hand," Daniel said.

∾∾

Forty minutes later, Nick Halliwell's sedan turned into the yard. Dylan, the big clumsy bay, whinnied when he saw his owner. Nick stroked him. "He's looking good," he said to Amy, his eyes taking in Dylan's shining coat and muscled neck and hindquarters.

"He's really improving," Amy said. "I'll take him out in the ring so you can see."

Daniel helped her get Dylan's tack.

"So how's that lovely show jumper of yours?" Nick asked as Amy came back.

"Pretty good," Amy said with a smile.

"Jumping out of his skin," Daniel said, swinging the saddle onto Dylan's broad back.

Amy caught Nick looking at Daniel curiously and realized she hadn't introduced them. "Nick, this is Daniel Lawson," she said. "He's a friend of mine. Daniel, this is Nick Halliwell."

"Pleased to meet you," Nick said, holding out his hand. As Daniel shook it, he frowned. "We haven't met before, have we? You look familiar."

"We've jumped together a few times," Daniel said.

"We were both in the Six Bar at the Meadowville show?"

Nick nodded. "Of course! I remember now. You ride that roan mare — what a great jumper. I haven't seen you on the circuit recently. How's she going?"

The air in the stall suddenly felt very still, almost stifling. Amy hardly dared look at Daniel.

"She, um . . ." Daniel cleared his throat. "She was put down last month. She broke a leg."

A mix of confusion and embarrassment washed over Nick's face. "I should have remembered. Amy did tell me at the time. I'm really sorry."

"It's OK," Daniel said quietly. "I understand."

There was an awkward pause.

"So what are you doing with yourself now, Daniel?" Nick asked, breaking the silence. "Did you ever find that working student place you were looking for?"

Daniel shook his head. "I'm working as a stable hand. At Green Briar."

"For the Grants?" Nick raised his eyebrows. "How's it going?"

"Not great," Daniel admitted, tightening Dylan's girth. "I'm actually thinking about moving on."

"Got a new position in mind?" Nick asked.

Daniel shook his head. "I guess I'll just take whatever comes up."

Nick looked thoughtfully at him and then patted

Dylan. "OK," he said to Amy. "Let's get this fellow working."

∾

As Amy rode Dylan around the ring on a loose rein to warm him up, she watched Nick and Daniel chatting by the gate. She was pleased that they seemed to be getting along. Daniel could sometimes be reserved and defensive with people he didn't know well — especially show types.

Feeling Dylan start to relax, she concentrated on his rhythm and, collecting the reins, began to walk him over a grid of six poles she had laid out on the ground earlier. The idea was that instead of simply riding the horse over them as you would do with traditional trotting poles, you also used the poles as a maze. By asking the horse to walk around the poles instead of over them, Amy knew Dylan would need to be more careful where he placed his feet. In addition, he had to bend his body first to the right and then to the left and really concentrate on what he was doing. It was part of a training system called T-team developed by a horsewoman named Linda Tellington-Jones. T-touch was part of the same approach.

As Dylan walked out of the maze of poles on the other side, Nick called out to her. "Why are you making him do that?"

"It's to help him become more aware of his body,"

Amy explained, riding Dylan over to the gate. "He has to really concentrate on where he is going, and that helps improve his general coordination and balance."

"He certainly looks more confident. Less clumsy," Nick said.

"He is," Amy replied. "I'll show you what he's like working on the bit in a minute."

She took Dylan through the maze several times, and then, when she was sure he was feeling relaxed and confident, she rode him away from the poles and asked him to trot on. Keeping him on a fairly short rein, she rode him through a series of transitions, circles, and serpentines. Whereas Dylan once would have found the more collected work difficult, he now easily accomplished what she asked.

"That's a big improvement," Nick said, looking impressed as she finally halted Dylan at the gate.

Daniel nodded. "I remember seeing him when he first arrived — I was staying here for a while. He was so awkward then."

"He's really coming along," Amy agreed, patting him. "He should be ready to come back to you soon, Nick."

Nick nodded. "That will be good. We can start jumping him then." He looked doubtful. "Though he'll probably be more of a pleasure horse than a successful show jumper. It's a pity. I bred him myself from one of my top mares."

Amy nodded. She had her doubts about Dylan's future as a show jumper, too. Dylan was a lovely horse, and his coordination was really improving, but top-level show jumpers needed superb balance and awareness. "He's very long in the back, isn't he?" she said, knowing that such a characteristic wasn't ideal in a show jumper. "And although he's improving, I think his rider will always have to keep his coordination in check with special exercises."

To her surprise, Daniel spoke up. "I think you're being too hasty. He's still a baby by show jumper standards. I know he looks long now, but sometimes big warmbloods take a few extra years to grow into their frames. With the correct work he should muscle up, his body shape will change, and, as that happens, his natural balance should come. He's got great hindquarters for a show jumper — really sloping, and his hocks are good and powerful. I wouldn't give up on him yet."

Amy looked at Nick, wondering how he'd take Daniel's comments. One of the things she liked about Daniel was that he wasn't awed by people and spoke his mind openly. But she knew that his forthright nature could take people off guard. To her relief, she saw that Nick didn't look offended. He was looking at Daniel with interest.

"It's strange you should say that," he said. "Dylan's dam did exactly that. She didn't have Dylan's coordination problems, but she was a big, gangly youngster. It was only when she hit seven that she really matured and started to perform. She turned into one of the best mares I've ever had. Not quite a top-class grand prix horse, but a brilliant puissant jumper." He looked at Dylan. "Maybe you're right. Maybe he does just need time."

"It's impossible to tell," Daniel said. "But if I were you, I wouldn't give up on him just yet."

Their eyes met and Nick smiled. "I might just take that advice, Daniel. Thank you. It's good to meet someone who has his own opinion." He turned to Amy. "May I have a ride on Dylan? See what he feels like?"

"Sure. He's your horse, after all," Amy said, dismounting.

While Nick rode Dylan around the ring, she joined Daniel at the gate.

"Nick's a really nice guy, isn't he?" Daniel said. "I've never really talked to him before. But he seems so genuine — not like some show jumpers."

"He is," Amy said, watching as Nick skillfully rode Dylan around the ring. "And he really cares about his horses. He takes training seriously."

"I like him," Daniel said.

❧

Nick left after riding Dylan. He was very pleased with the young horse's progress and agreed to visit again the following week. At that point, he'd set a day when Dylan should return to his stable.

Daniel stayed for brunch and then helped with the other horses. At the end of the afternoon, Amy walked with him to his pickup.

"You take care now," he said to her. "Don't work too hard. When's your next show?"

"Next weekend," she replied. "It's at East Creek. I'm going in the High Junior Jumpers — it'll be our first time in the elite division."

"Storm will hardly even notice the height difference," Daniel said, climbing into his truck. "He's one hell of a horse, Amy."

"I know." Amy smiled.

"Well, good luck," he said, starting the engine. "I'll give you a call soon."

❧

That night, Tim Fleming, the girls' father, phoned. He lived in Australia. He had been out of Amy's and Lou's lives for twelve years, until Lou had located him six months ago. She and Amy were now in regular contact with him.

"How's Storm going?" he asked Amy.

"Great," Amy enthused. "We won again last weekend."

"Junior Jumpers?"

"Yep. The low division, but we're going in the higher division for the first time next Saturday."

"Excellent," Tim said. Amy could hear the smile in his voice. "Soon you'll be competing in intermediate and open."

"I wish," Amy said.

"What's all this *I wish* business?" her dad asked. "You have the talent. You're going to make it into the big time with Storm, Amy. I can see it now. World Championships, Pan-Am Games . . ."

"Dad!" Amy said, laughing. "Be realistic!"

"You've got the right horse for it," her dad said. "If you want it enough, I know you can make it happen."

Amy didn't say anything. She just thought about what he'd said. *If you want it enough . . .*

How much *did* she want success with Storm — enough to make it her one goal in life? Enough to give up her work at Heartland?

"Amy?" her dad said.

"Yeah, I'm here," she told him.

"Listen, if you need anything for Storm, just let me know," he said. "I know how expensive competing can be. Soon you'll be wanting to travel farther to shows. You might want to do the Florida circuit next winter, and as you move up, you'll be having to stay at events for days at a time. It'll cost money, but I'm more than happy to fund you. I'd like to help."

"Thanks," Amy said. She wished that it was just a question of money, but it was much, much more. She thought for a moment about discussing her Heartland and show-jumping dilemma with her dad, but the instant the thought had formed she knew there was no point. When he was younger, his life had been totally focused on show jumping. He'd never understand how she could want to do both.

"Is there something wrong?" Tim asked as the silence went on.

"No," Amy said quickly. "No, nothing's wrong. So — so how are you, Dad? How's business going, and how are Helena and Lily?"

They started to chat about Tim's work and about his new wife, Helena, and their baby daughter.

When Amy finally put down the phone, she stood for a while in the silence of the kitchen. She walked to the window and looked out. Jake, Dancer, and Storm were dozing over their stable doors, their heads nodding, their eyes half closed. It was such a peaceful scene that Amy felt a warm rush of pride. Her mom had made Heartland what it was, and now she and Ty were continuing the work.

But what about her show-jumping dreams? If she was going to make it to the top, she was going to have to start traveling with Storm. She would have to leave Heartland for days at a time to compete in shows in other states.

Her heart clenched, and in an instant she knew she couldn't do it. She couldn't leave Heartland and the horses that needed her. *I belong here,* she thought.

But if she didn't travel, then she and Storm could never get beyond a certain level on the show circuit. She would be stuck in the lower divisions, forced to watch while people like Ashley moved on and up. Amy knew she wouldn't be able to bear that, either.

"What do I do?" she whispered, looking out at the quiet yard.

But there was no easy answer.

Chapter Six

Over the next few days, Amy hardly had time to think about the future. Instead, she concentrated on the work at hand. Her patience and time with Willow were paying off. The pony didn't seem to be suffering any aftereffects from her fall. By Wednesday, she was happily letting Amy tie her up, groom her, and put a blanket on.

As Amy eased the blanket off Willow's back and watched the little pony standing quietly, she felt a warm glow of happiness. To see a pony that had once been so terrified now learning to trust made every minute she had spent seem worthwhile.

"She's doing great."

Amy turned and saw Ty watching a little way off.

"She is, isn't she?" Amy smiled, knowing Ty would share her satisfaction. Putting the blanket down quietly, she moved to the pony's head and untied her. "Why don't you try coming closer?" she suggested. "She should be better now."

Amy massaged Willow's neck with T-touch circles as Ty walked closer, his eyes lowered, his body language as unthreatening as possible. Amy could see Willow watching him, but the pony didn't try to move away. As Ty reached Amy's side, Willow lifted her head slightly. "It's OK, girl," Amy murmured.

Ty stood quietly, and Willow gradually started to relax again. All the while, Amy's fingers worked on Willow's neck. Seeing the wariness leave her eyes, Amy had an idea.

"Put your hand on mine," she said softly to Ty.

Ty didn't need to ask why. He placed his fingers lightly over hers. Willow tensed slightly, but as Amy massaged her, she relaxed again.

Ty began to massage the pony's neck alongside Amy. She didn't know how long they stood there, but little by little the world slipped slowly back into her consciousness and she opened her eyes. She looked up and met Ty's eyes. Then, without speaking, she moved her fingers out from under his so that he alone was touching Willow. She stepped quietly back. The pony watched her move away but allowed Ty to keep on massaging her skin with his strong, sensitive fingers.

Delight swept through Amy. Willow was finally

allowing someone else to touch her. She was slowly accepting other people.

After a few minutes, Ty patted Willow and stepped back. His eyes met Amy's, and she stepped forward and impulsively kissed him on the cheek. "Thank you," she said to him.

Ty smiled warmly. "Anytime."

❧

All day, Amy was filled with happiness, thinking of Willow's improvement and how Ty had helped with her treatment. *There really is nothing like working with damaged horses,* she thought as she rode Storm across the lawn that afternoon. *Not even winning in the ring.*

Suddenly, the sound of the phone ringing brought her back to the present. A moment later, the back door opened, and Lou looked out. "Amy, Daniel's on the phone. Here, I'll take Storm for you." Lou took the reins and, dismounting, Amy went into the house.

"Hey, Daniel, how are you?" she said, picking up the phone.

"Great!"

Hearing the excitement in Daniel's voice, Amy said quickly, "What's up?"

"I just got the best news," Daniel said. "Nick Halliwell called me this morning and offered me a job. As a working pupil!"

"Daniel, that's wonderful!" Amy exclaimed.

"I went to visit his stable this afternoon," Daniel went on. "It's amazing — top-level horses, nice people, and Nick — well, he's great. I watched him working a range of horses from a green four-year-old to Luna, his grand prix jumper. I'm going to learn so much from him. It's hard to believe. After everything that's happened . . ."

Amy was delighted. "Daniel, I'm so happy for you. Nick's fantastic. You'll love working for him."

"I know." Daniel's voice dropped. "I — I just wish Amber could be going with me."

There was a pause. Amy didn't know what to say.

Daniel sighed. "I always thought when I got the chance that Amber and I would make it to the top together. Now things are starting to happen, only it's without her. It's not the same dream I've had all these years."

Amy hesitated. "Dreams change," she said quietly. "They have to."

"Yeah, I guess so," Daniel said. She heard him take a breath, and then he changed the subject. "I can't wait to leave Green Briar."

"When do you start at Nick's?" Amy asked.

"I'm moving there tomorrow," Daniel replied. "I start work on Friday."

"Wow!" Amy said in astonishment. "That's quick. Doesn't Val want you to work through your notice?"

"No."

Amy heard a note of hesitation in Daniel's voice and had a feeling that he wasn't telling her something. "Daniel?" she said.

"I — um — kind of got myself fired," he admitted.

"What?" Amy said in astonishment.

"Well, when I got back from Nick's, I went to find Mrs. Grant to give her my notice. She was with Duke. She was getting one of the grooms to try to lift his feet and another to shoot his hindquarters with a pellet gun every time he lunged backward."

Amy gasped. "What? That's awful!"

"He was terrified. He was about to rip the cross ties from the wall. I lost my temper and told her that if she didn't stop I'd call the ASPCA. Then I told her what I thought of her brutal training methods. She said she wanted me off the yard within twenty-four hours."

"What about Duke?" Amy asked.

"He's a total wreck. He won't let anyone near him. I tried to enter his stall but thought better of it. I heard Val say she's going to sell him."

"But how will she find anyone to buy him?" Amy said.

"She's just going to send him to a sale," Daniel said. "She'll cut her losses and sell him as unwarranted."

Amy's heart sank. Unwarranted horses usually went for glue. She thought of the handsome bay gelding. It was devastating to think what Val Grant had done to him. An idea came to Amy. "Find out when she's going to sell him," she said quickly. "And let me know."

"Why?" Daniel said. "Are you thinking of buying him?"

"I'll have to talk to Lou," Amy replied, her mind racing. "But we have the money I won on Storm the other week. So it's a possibility."

"That would be great," Daniel said eagerly. "I'm sure he's not vicious. He was fine when he first came to Green Briar. If you figure him out, you could sell him and make yourself a healthy profit."

"That wouldn't be why I'd do it," Amy said.

"I know that," Daniel said. "But he has won a lot, so he's well known. You could get a good price for him if he was back on the eventing circuit and going well. Look, I'll try and find out Green Briar's plans for him before I leave tomorrow. I'll give you a call when I know something more."

"Thanks," Amy said.

She put the phone down and took a deep breath. Now she had to talk to Lou.

❧

Lou was in Storm's stable, rubbing him down. Amy quickly told her all about Duke and how Val had treated him, about Daniel losing his temper, and finally how Duke was now going to an auction to be sold as unwarranted.

"Poor animal," Lou said, shaking her head in sympathy.

Amy hesitated, wondering how to break her plan to Lou, but Lou spoke before she could say anything. "We should buy him, Amy," she said quickly. "Then you and Ty could help him here. It might be his only chance."

Amy stared at her.

"You don't think it's a good idea," Lou said, looking at her uncertainly.

Amy found her tongue. "No! I do, I definitely do," she burst out. "In fact, I was about to ask whether we could do just that. I thought we could use the money I won at the show."

"Good idea," Lou said. "It's money we weren't expecting to have, so I haven't budgeted to use it for anything in particular. Why not put it toward this?" She put down the currycomb she was using. "Come on, let's find Ty and Grandpa and see what they say."

They hurried across the yard to where Grandpa and Ty were rehanging one of the field gates.

"Hi," Ty said, looking up as they approached.

Seeing them both, Grandpa put down the gate. "Something up?" he asked.

"We need to talk to you about something," Amy said, glancing at Lou. "It's about this horse at Green Briar. . . ."

She told them all about Duke and how he was going to a sale. "I really think we should help him," she finished. "Lou does, too."

Lou nodded. "It sounds like Heartland is the best place for him. We want to buy him, but we thought we'd see what you both thought of the idea."

"I definitely think we should if we can afford it," Ty said immediately. "It sounds like Green Briar has been a nightmare for him."

"I agree, but we should think about the time he'll need," Grandpa advised, looking slightly worried. "You're pushed to the limit as it is, Amy."

Ty spoke up. "I'm more than happy to take the lead on this one. I know Amy doesn't have much time at the moment, but I can fit in another horse."

"Thanks, Ty," Amy said gratefully. She looked at Grandpa. "Well? Can we buy him?"

Grandpa nodded. "Sure. If Lou thinks we've got the money, then it's all right by me."

"Thank you!" Amy cried, hugging him. "Thank you so much!"

❧

Amy rushed to call Daniel back and told him the good news.

"That's great," he said. "I've found out that the Grants

are planning on sending Duke to a sale next week. But I could always ask her if she'll sell him to me. It would save her the cost of taking him to the sale and paying the auction fee."

"You think she'd let you buy him?" Amy asked.

"I think so," Daniel replied. "She just wants him off the yard, and selling him to me will save her money. I'll just tell her I really like him and want to take him with me when I leave. She'll think I'm crazy and will consider it good riddance."

"How much do you think she'll want for him?" Amy asked.

Daniel named what he thought was a good offer.

"We can afford that," Amy said.

"How should I get the money from you?" Daniel asked. "I have a lot to get done before I leave. I should try to talk to Val today."

"I'll get Lou to withdraw the money from the bank, and we'll meet you in the Green Briar parking lot in an hour. Then you can buy him from Val and bring him here tomorrow in your trailer. Will that work?"

"I think so," Daniel said. "Look, I'll go and talk to her now. If she doesn't agree, I'll call you."

An hour later, Amy and Lou drove into the Green Briar parking lot. Amy looked around anxiously for Daniel. She didn't want to get out of the truck in case Val saw her.

A group of children was standing in the nearest training ring. Amy's attention was caught by their smart olive breeches and shiny leather boots. They didn't have a mark on them. One by one, their horses were led into the ring and they mounted. Without so much as a word to the stable hands, they turned their horses to the rail for their lesson.

Lou shook her head. "Did you see that? Not one of those kids thanked the stable hands. They just took their horses as if they expected to have people running around taking care of them."

Amy remembered the woman she'd seen riding last time she'd visited Green Briar. She, too, had simply handed her horse over to the stable hand without a word of thanks.

"I bet they don't even know what a grooming brush looks like," Amy said. "They just get on when the horse is ready, and when they've finished riding they hand it back. No way could I do that." She stopped.

A small voice spoke in the back of her mind. *Isn't that what you're doing with Storm? Yesterday Lou untacked him for you. And she's been grooming him.*

"Here's Daniel," Lou said, interrupting her thoughts.

Amy turned. Daniel was hurrying toward the car.

"Here's the money," Lou said, passing it to him through the window. "Is everything still a go?"

Daniel nodded. "Mrs. Grant's agreed I can buy him.

She clearly thinks I'm insane, but she jumped at the chance to get rid of him without the hassle and expense of the sale." He looked around. "Look, I'd better go. I'll see you tomorrow."

Lou smiled. "See you then!"

At nine o'clock the next morning, Daniel arrived with Duke. "He wasn't easy to load," he said. "He's not very fond of people at the moment."

"I can't say I blame him," Ty said. "I don't think I'd like people if they shot me in the butt with a pellet gun."

As they eased down the ramp, Duke gave a warning kick.

"He's not really mean," Daniel assured. "He's just scared. Where's his stall?"

"In the front block, next to Jake," Amy said.

Daniel went into the trailer. There was a brief struggle as Duke threatened to bite Daniel, but Daniel expertly untied the lead rope and led the bay gelding out to the lawn. When Duke saw Amy and the others, he pinned his ears back. He looked wary and untrusting.

Amy felt incredibly sorry for him. "Poor thing."

Ty squeezed her shoulder. "We'll get through to him in the end," he said. "Things will get better for him. I know they will."

❧

Daniel left for Nick's, promising to call them in a few days.

"Good luck on Saturday," he told Amy as he got into his pickup.

It took Amy a moment to realize the significance of Saturday. The show! Her first time in High Junior Jumpers. "Thanks." She grinned.

"You'd almost forgotten about it, hadn't you?" Ben said to her as Daniel drove away.

"Yeah," she admitted. "So much has been happening."

"And now you're even busier," Ben said, glancing at Duke's stall. "I don't know how you're going to find time for it all."

"Me, neither," Amy admitted with an uncertain smile. "Come on, let's get the horses in."

❧

Over the next few days, Ty spent hours with Duke, and Amy found herself busier than ever. Despite the fact that Willow now tolerated other people handling her, the only person she really trusted was Amy. Amy spent a lot of time trying to build up her confidence.

On Friday, the weather turned again, and Amy decided that it would be safer to keep Willow in the barn overnight in case the wind upset her. She settled the pony in the stall next to Sundance, who was back to health after his bout of colic.

"You're going to be OK, girl," she said, massaging Willow's muzzle with diluted lavender oil. The smell of the oil and the touch of Amy's fingers seemed to soothe the pony slightly, and she relaxed enough to pull at her hay net.

Amy let herself out of the stall. It was seven o'clock, and she still had to get Storm ready for the show. Lou had groomed him, but Amy wanted to wash his tail and legs. Quickly, she made her way down the yard and got some water and shampoo.

Storm nuzzled her as she came into the stall. Amy kissed his face. She felt like she had hardly seen him for days. All she did with him was ride, give him a quick brush over, and put him back in his stall or out in the field.

"I'm getting to be like one of those riders at Green Briar, aren't I, Storm?" she said sadly.

Storm rubbed his face against her arm.

His obvious delight at seeing her made Amy feel even more guilty. "I wish I had more time to spend with you. I really do," she told him. "Tomorrow will be different, I promise. It'll be just you and me at the show all day. No one else. Just you and me."

🔖

The wind was still blowing strongly when Amy got up the next morning, and the first thing she did when she went out was check on Willow. The little pony was looking jittery. She whinnied when she saw Amy and kicked the stall door.

Amy knew she should really get a move on and start braiding Storm, but she couldn't leave Willow in such a nervous state.

Going into the pony's stall, she started massaging her lips and muzzle with T-touch circles. Slowly, Willow calmed down, and at last Amy felt happy enough to leave her.

Her grandfather was already mucking out the front stable block.

"Thanks," Amy called out as she headed for Storm's stall.

"No problem," Grandpa called back, pressing down the straw in the wheelbarrow. "I hope this wind blows over before you get to the show," he said.

"Me, too," Amy agreed. "It isn't going to be fun jumping in a wind this strong." She opened Storm's door. "Hey, boy, looking forward to the show?"

He snorted and came over for some attention.

By the time Ben and Ty arrived, Storm was braided and groomed.

"Will you be ready to leave in half an hour?" Ben asked her.

"Should be," Amy replied. Putting her grooming kit away, she went to help Ty feed the horses.

❧

"Willow seems wound up," Ty said when he returned to the feed room with the empty feed buckets a little while later. "She didn't eat any of her breakfast."

Amy looked up from the hay nets. "I was hoping she might have calmed down by now," she said, frowning. "I'll go and massage her with some lavender oil — it worked last night."

"But you've got to finish getting ready for the show. I'll do it," Ty said.

Amy hesitated. She needed to load her stuff into the trailer, but she knew that Willow would calm down much quicker for her than for Ty. "Thanks, Ty, but it's probably easier if I do it. She's more likely to relax with me."

Grabbing the bottle of lavender oil from the feed room, Amy hurried to the barn. Willow was pacing around her stall, her ears flickering. Pouring a little oil into her hand, she began to massage Willow's muzzle as she had the night before. Gradually, Willow quieted down.

"Amy! We should go!" Ben called from the barn door.

"Just five more minutes," she called back, wanting to make sure Willow was fully calm before she left.

"We're running late as it is," Ben said, coming down the aisle. "I've loaded your stuff, but we should get going."

Amy hesitated, feeling torn. She really didn't want to leave the pony.

"I'll put Storm in the trailer for you," Ben said.

"It's all right. I'm coming!" Amy said. She kissed Willow's nose. "You be good now, Willow. I'll be back later."

The pony followed her to the door, nickering anxiously.

As Amy hurried toward the barn door, she heard Willow whinny after her. She felt a stab of guilt. She shouldn't be going. Willow needed her. She should stay behind.

Chapter Seven

"And now, in the ring in class seventy-five, Amy Fleming riding Summer Storm," the loudspeaker crackled.

There was a smattering of applause. Giving Storm a quick pat, Amy trotted him into the ring. *Concentrate,* she told herself. *Focus.*

But it was hard. From the moment she and Ben had left Heartland, all she had been able to think about was Willow. Every instinct in her body seemed to be telling her she should be at home.

Storm's hooves barely seemed to touch the short green grass. He looked around eagerly at the brightly painted jumps and the white stands, and he pulled at the bit in excitement.

"Steady now," Amy said. She forced her thoughts to

focus on him. Leaning forward, she let Storm swing into a canter. The starting bell rang.

Turning Storm toward the first fence, Amy felt her mind drain of everything but Storm and the course of jumps in front of her. All the guilt and the stress she had been feeling faded into nothingness, and she was left with a wonderful sense of peace. "Come on, boy," she whispered, her eyes fixed on the first fence. "We can do it!"

Lengthening his stride and meeting the jump perfectly, Storm soared over it. Moving as one with him, Amy guided Storm skillfully over jump after jump. The grass and crowds were a mere blur. Her whole being was focused on the horse beneath her and the jumps they had to clear.

As they landed safely after the last fence with a clear round, the crowd clapped loudly. Vigorously patting Storm's neck, Amy rode out of the ring, her eyes shining with excitement and delight.

"He just gets better!" Ben said, meeting her outside the ring.

"He's wonderful!" Amy said, dismounting.

Storm rubbed the side of his face against Amy's chest. She scratched his forehead. "You're the best," she told him.

He snorted and looked around. He looked so happy to

be at a show that Amy had to smile. "He is such a competitor."

Ben nodded. "I know you can't see him when he's in the ring, but it's like there's a light that goes on inside him as soon as he sees the jumps. I'm sure that's why he's such a wonderful jumper — he just loves to show off."

Ben's cell phone rang. Looking surprised, he dug it out of his pocket. "Ben Stillman. Oh, hi, Ty. Yeah, yeah. I'll get her, she's here."

He handed the phone to Amy. She took it quickly. Ty! Why was he calling? All the thoughts that had drained from her mind when she was in the ring suddenly came swarming back.

"Ty," she said in alarm. "What is it?"

"It's Willow," Ty said. "The wind blew down a branch that fell on the barn roof, and the commotion has really upset her."

"Do you want me to come back?" Amy asked. She looked at Storm standing so eagerly beside her, and her heart sank. She would miss the jump-off, and Ben would have to scratch from his class.

"I think you should," Ty said. "She won't let me near her, and she's kicking her stall like crazy. I'm worried she's going to hurt herself."

He didn't have to say any more. "We'll head back right away," Amy told him.

She saw Ben look at her in surprise. She handed the phone to him. "Talk to Ty."

As Ty explained, Amy looked at Storm. "I'm sorry," she said.

To her relief, Ben was in complete agreement that they should go back. "There'll be other shows," he said. "You take Storm back and get his legs wrapped. I'll talk to the steward and let him know you won't be in the jump-off and to scratch Red from his class. I wasn't looking forward to jumping in this wind anyway."

Amy walked Storm back to the trailer. He followed her eagerly enough, but when she started taking his tack off and getting his traveling boots out he nudged her in a puzzled way.

"I know, Storm," she said. "You think we should be warming up for the jump-off, but we can't. We've got to go home. I'm really sorry."

For the first time ever, Storm refused to go up the ramp into the trailer. He looked back toward the ring as if he were trying to tell her she'd forgotten something. Amy understood, but there was nothing she could do. They had to get back to Heartland.

"Come on, Storm, please," she said, clicking her tongue and trying again.

Storm pulled back, his muzzle lifted, but after a moment he walked resignedly up the ramp.

⸘

Amy thought about Willow all the way home. She never should have left that morning. Her instincts had been right. The second Ben stopped the pickup, Amy jumped out. There was no sign of Ty — or anyone. She headed for the barn. Reaching it, she heard raised voices and the sound of hooves kicking wood.

"Steady, girl! Steady!"

"Easy there!"

"Should we call Scott?"

Amy raced down the aisle. She could hear the alarm in Grandpa's and Ty's voices. What had happened? She saw Grandpa standing outside Willow's stall. Ty was in the doorway.

"Amy, thank goodness you're here," Grandpa said, seeing her. "Willow's put her back hoof through the wall, and it's stuck."

Amy stopped beside Ty and immediately saw what the problem was. In her panic, Willow had kicked so hard that one of her back hooves had gone straight through the wooden paneling. The pony was trying desperately to pull it free, but her fetlock was wedged between two boards. Her eyes rolled, her ears were flat back, and blood was spraying the wall.

Amy didn't stop to think. "Shush, Willow. Easy does it," she said, going into the stall.

Seeing Amy, Willow let out a whicker of recognition and tried to steady her back leg.

"It's all right." Amy breathed. Holding out her hand, she stepped closer to the pony. "I'm here. I'll look after you."

Willow's sides trembled. Reaching out with her nose, she touched Amy's hand with her muzzle. Amy stroked the pony's face and neck. "It's OK, girl," she said quickly. "Everything's going to be OK."

Willow pulled at her hoof anxiously.

"Easy now," Amy said. "I'll get you free." She moved slowly around to the wall. Willow's foot was caught behind a piece of wood that had splintered when she had kicked the hole but then had fallen back when she tried to pull her foot in the opposite direction. Using both hands, Amy pried the broken wood away from the hole. "There, girl," she said.

Willow heaved her leg and the hoof came out of the hole. Her fetlock was scraped and bleeding, and there was a nasty slice above her hoof, but at least she was now free. As Amy moved around to her front side, Willow buried her face against Amy's chest and stood there as if trying to hide from the world.

"What happened?" Amy said to Ty.

"I was trying to calm her, and she panicked even more," he replied. "That's when she put her foot through the wall."

Amy stroked Willow's hot neck. "I'm glad we got back when we did."

"Me, too," said Ty. "She just got it caught about ten minutes ago, but there was no way she was letting me near her."

"I've got the first aid kit here," Grandpa said quietly.

"I'll let her calm down, and then we'll see to her cuts," Amy said. "Maybe it would be best if you left me with her for a while."

They both moved away.

Amy whispered, "Oh, Willow. What are we going to do with you?" She started to massage the pony's forehead with T-touch circles. The pony sighed in relief.

After Willow had calmed down slightly, Amy got some water to bathe the cuts on her leg. Ben had unloaded Storm, and the gelding was now looking over his stable door. He whinnied eagerly when he saw Amy walking past with the water.

"Sorry, boy," Amy said, "but I have to look after Willow right now."

As she continued up the yard, Storm whinnied again. Amy stopped and looked back. He was staring at her in confusion. Amy felt awful. He obviously couldn't understand why she was ignoring him.

She glanced at the bucket of water in her hand. No,

she decided, as hard as it was, she knew Willow needed her more than he did at this point.

The cuts on the pony's leg were mainly just scrapes and scratches, and none of them was deep enough to need stitches. As she dressed the wounds, Amy kept thinking about Storm — the sound of his whinny, the confusion in his eyes. She felt so guilty. She was being so unfair to Storm, to Willow. *What am I doing?* she thought.

"Um — Amy," Ty said, coming to the stall door. "Would it help you if I took Storm's braids out?"

"No. Yes. Oh, I don't know, Ty," Amy cried out, all her frustration and confusion bursting out of her in a sudden rush. She covered her face with her hands.

"Amy? What's wrong?" Ty said quickly.

Amy dug the heels of her fists into her forehead. "I can't do this any longer, Ty," she said in an anguished voice. "I can't be in two places at once." The words came out before she could stop them. "I'm going to stop competing Storm."

As soon as the words left her she wanted to snatch them back but, at the same time, she felt an overpowering feeling of relief. She'd finally said it. Finally admitted that she just couldn't go on — not like she had been.

"Hey," Ty said gently, coming into the stall. "It's just been a bad day."

"No, Ty," Amy interrupted. "It's more than that. It's been this way for weeks. I'm being split in two."

"But giving up competing altogether" — Ty's eyes searched her face — "couldn't you just cut back on the number of shows you go to?"

Amy desperately wanted to say yes, to cling to the hope that she could still compete with Storm, but she knew better. "It wouldn't work. You know me. I'd always want to do more, to try and move up a level, and so would Storm."

Ty didn't argue. He obviously knew she was right. She shook her head. "It's shows or Heartland, Ty. I can't keep doing both. It's not fair to you or the horses or Storm." Her voice faltered as she thought about Storm, about how he would feel never competing in a show again.

Just then, Ben came into the barn. "How's Willow?" He caught sight of the unhappiness on Amy's face and frowned. "Is she in bad shape?"

Amy swallowed. Telling Ty that she was giving up shows was one thing. She knew he would understand, but telling Ben would make it seem public and official. "I" — she forced the words out — "I'm going to give up taking Storm to shows." She waited for his reaction.

Ben stared at her in astonishment. "What did you say?"

Amy felt empty inside. Never to go in the showring

again! Never to fly around a course of jumps like she and Storm had that day. *It's the only way,* she told herself. She looked Ben in the eye. "I can't do it, Ben," she said. "Not anymore. I'm needed here."

She felt Ty's hand squeeze her shoulder in silent support.

"But — but —" Ben seemed lost for words. "What about Storm?" he said at last. "What will you do with him?"

Amy frowned. "Nothing. I'm going to keep him here, of course. I'll still ride him — just not at shows."

"But you can't do that!" Ben exclaimed. "He's way too talented to be wasted that way! You know that."

An image of Storm, full of vigor and anticipation as he waited to enter the ring, came into Amy's mind, but she pushed it away. "He'll get used to not competing," she said. She stood up, hoping to avoid further arguments from Ben. "He'll just have to," she said desperately as she pushed past him.

Storm was looking out over his door. He whinnied when he saw her, and she went into his stall and put her arms around his strong warm neck.

As he nuzzled her back, tears sprang to her eyes. "I'm sorry, Storm," she whispered. "I really am." Swallowing hard, she stepped back and stroked his handsome face. "You'll be happy," she said. "We might not go to shows, but we'll go out on the trails every day. No more schooling. No more boring circles and transitions. You'll like that."

Storm pushed at her with his nose, not understanding, just pleased that she was there.

Amy rested her forehead against his neck. *He'll be fine,* she told herself. *He'll be happy. I know he will.*

Chapter Eight

"You're not going to shows anymore?" Lou stared at her. "But why?"

"Because I don't have time for them," Amy told her.

Grandpa put down the bridle he was mending. "Are you sure about this, Amy?"

"Yes," she said firmly. "I'm giving up the show scene." It got easier to say each time.

"But what will you do with Storm?" Grandpa said.

"Why does everyone keep asking me that?" Amy demanded. "I'll just keep him for riding on the trails, that's all."

"But, honey, he's been bred to compete," Grandpa said. "It's in his blood."

"So? What else can I do?" Amy said.

Lou glanced at Grandpa.

Amy suddenly didn't want to hear what either of them might say. "There isn't any other option," she said swiftly. "Storm stays here and becomes a pleasure horse. I'll still jump him from time to time. There's nothing wrong with that. That's all most horses do!" Her voice rose defensively.

"It's all right. Don't get upset," Grandpa said quietly.

"I'm not getting upset!" Amy exclaimed. "I just can't see why everyone's making such a big deal about this." She shook her head. "I'm going to my room," she said, and she walked out of the kitchen and up the stairs.

Reaching her bedroom, she sank down on her bed. She knew she couldn't keep competing, so Storm would just have to get used to not going to shows. It was the *only* thing she could do, so why was everyone acting like there was some other option? There wasn't one — not unless she *sold* Storm.

The thought had barely formed before Amy was pushing it away. No. Storm was hers. Well, technically he was hers and Lou's, but he was hers in spirit. He loved her. They belonged together. They were a team. She shut her eyes and saw his handsome face, heard his whinny, imagined him nuzzling her arm. She shook her head. No. She could never part with him. He didn't need to go to shows because he'd be happy just to be at Heartland with her. She was sure of it.

She heard the phone ringing downstairs. A minute later, Lou shouted to her.

"Amy! It's Daniel!"

"Coming!" She sighed.

Lou met her on the staircase and handed her the phone.

"Hello," Amy said, going back upstairs. "How's it going at Nick's?"

"I really like it here." Daniel's words were reserved, but his voice rang with enthusiasm. "I'm riding some amazing horses. Nick likes to designate two or three young horses to his working pupils and, even though I'm supposed to be just a stable hand for the time being, he's put me in charge of two horses already. I basically groom and ride them and help Nick figure out a competition schedule for them. It's like having my own horses."

"That's great! What are the other people there like?" Amy asked.

"They're really nice. There's a sense of team spirit. It's kind of weird — it couldn't be more different from Green Briar."

"Well, that's good news," Amy said.

"How's Duke doing?" he asked.

Amy had to think for a moment. "He's OK," she said. "Ty's been working with him. He seems to be slowly realizing we're not going to hurt him."

"And what about the show?" Daniel said. "How was that?"

"Oh, not great," Amy replied. "Storm jumped clear, but Ben and I had to leave before the jump-off. Willow had an accident and wouldn't let Ty near her."

"That's too bad," Daniel said. "At least you've got other shows coming up. You're going to Marriott Park next weekend, aren't you? They pull in a lot of top horses."

"Well, I won't be there." Amy took a deep breath and broke the news to him. "Storm and I are not going to shows anymore."

"You can't be serious," Daniel said. "You're so good together."

"I don't have a choice," Amy told him. "I can't keep showing *and* run Heartland."

"Maybe you should get someone else to show Storm for you," Daniel said.

Amy hesitated. She hadn't considered that possibility. She tried to imagine what it would be like to watch the trailer heading down the Heartland driveway with Storm inside, knowing someone else would be riding him.

"How about asking Ben?" Daniel continued. "It would be easy for him to take Storm and Red in different divisions."

"No." Amy was already shaking her head. Ben was a great rider, but he was too authoritative. He rode with a firm hand and a strong seat, taking control and telling horses what to do. His style suited a lot of horses that would take confidence from his strong leadership. But Amy knew it wasn't right for Storm. He liked a very light touch, a sensitive rider. "I don't think Ben and Storm would be good for each other."

"Well, I could ride him for you," Daniel suggested.

For an instant, the memory of Daniel riding Storm around the Heartland ring flashed into Amy's mind. There was no doubt Storm had enjoyed being ridden by Daniel. But she still couldn't picture someone else showing him. A realization filled Amy's mind, clear and definite — and she admitted the truth to herself. She simply couldn't bear the thought of Storm going to shows without her — not with Ben, not with Daniel, not with anyone. If Storm was in the ring, then she wanted to be the one riding him.

"Well?" Daniel said when she didn't speak.

Amy felt awkward. She didn't want to admit she was being selfish. "Thanks for offering," she said quickly. "But I'm not sure it would work, Daniel. You're going to have your hands full at Nick's. Soon you'll be riding in shows for him, and then you won't have any extra time to compete Storm."

"I guess that's true," Daniel admitted. He sighed. "I just wish there was something you could do."

Amy spoke positively. "Storm will be fine. He'll get to

play in the fields and go out on the trails. It's not a bad life."

"But is it the right life for Storm?" Daniel asked.

Amy didn't say anything.

"You never know," Daniel said. "Things might be different next year. You might change your mind."

"Maybe," Amy said, but she knew she wouldn't. If the choice was between shows and Heartland — well, there wasn't a choice.

Amy tried not to think about her decision. She found that if she concentrated on working she could almost forget that she wasn't preparing for the next show, the next challenge. She could almost believe that next week or the week after, she and Storm would be setting off in the trailer again and that Storm would be flying around a course of jumps. No one mentioned her decision to her. However, on Tuesday night, Lou did ask in an almost too casual way if she had spoken to Tim since the weekend. Amy hadn't. She was dreading it. She knew how disappointed her dad was going to be when he heard the news.

Amy threw herself into her work. It wasn't hard to keep herself busy. For a start, she was determined to help Willow overcome her fear of noises.

"She can't keep panicking every time she hears something flap or bang," she said to Ty as they groomed the little bay pony the next day. "She'll never be safe to be ridden."

"I know," Ty said. He looked thoughtful. "How about we set up a kind of obstacle course for her?"

"An obstacle course?" Amy echoed, wondering what he meant.

"You know, a series of things that might make her nervous — flags, cones, bags, plastic sacks. We probably won't be able to get her close to them at first, but hopefully as she starts to realize that they're not going to hurt her, she'll become more confident. Eventually, she should get so used to them that they won't bother her anymore."

"It's a great idea," Amy said enthusiastically. "Let's try it this afternoon."

At lunchtime, they set out a course of obstacles in one of the smaller paddocks. They placed down a grid of poles, stuck a flag in a cone, found a bucket that could be rattled, put a plastic bag on a stick, and put a sheet of plastic on the ground, weighted down with stones.

"Come on, Willow," Amy said, leading the pony into the pasture.

Willow walked a few paces into the field and then stopped and stared at the obstacles. Amy stood beside her, letting the pony take her time. "Nothing's going to hurt you," she told the pony while stroking her neck. "I promise."

As Willow started to relax, Amy walked to the end of the lead rope. She didn't pull Willow or encourage her. She just waited. After five minutes, Willow stepped forward of her own accord. Amy started to walk around the outside of the pasture. She held the lead rope at the end and Willow followed her. Every time they had completed a circuit of the paddock, Amy led Willow slightly closer to the obstacles. Occasionally, Willow would tense nervously. Amy would listen to her fear and let her stop. Each time, she waited calmly for Willow to relax again and then led her on.

After half an hour the pony was walking about eight feet away from the obstacles.

"I won't take her any closer today," Amy said to Ty, who was watching by the gate. "I don't want to push it too quickly and frighten her."

Ty nodded his agreement. "You've had an audience," he said, pointing to the next field.

Solitaire was watching curiously over the fence, and it gave Amy an idea. "I know Solly's not going to be backed for several years yet," she said, "but couldn't we do the obstacle course with her, too? It'll be good for her to get used to things like this now. And she's so confident I can't imagine she'll be fazed."

Amy was right. The next day Ty led the foal into the paddock alongside Willow. The youngster hardly even looked twice at the poles or the flag or the flapping plastic bag, but she did stick her head into the bucket to see if there was any food inside.

Solly's confidence seemed to have a good effect on Willow. Seeing Solitaire exploring things so readily, the bay pony cautiously edged closer.

"That's great!" Ty said as Willow walked up to the bucket and began to nose at it.

Amy nodded, delighted at Willow's new confidence. "Working the two of them together seems to be effective."

They let the two ponies touch noses. "They like each other," Amy said. "Why don't we put them out in the same field? Now that Willow's reliable to catch, we don't need to put her out on her own anymore."

"Good idea," Ty agreed.

After they had finished with the obstacle course, they turned Solitaire and Willow out together. The two youngsters trotted away and settled down to graze.

"They look happy," Amy said.

Ty smiled. "They do." He took Amy's hand, and they started to walk toward the barn. "So, how are you feeling?" he asked.

"What do you mean?" Amy asked, knowing full well he was talking about her decision not to compete anymore, but stalling for time.

"About Storm," Ty persisted. "Have you changed your mind?"

"No," Amy said, not wanting to talk about it. "But I'm fine about it."

And is Storm? a little voice asked in her head. She ignored it. Storm would be fine, too.

To her relief, Ty dropped the subject.

As they reached the front stable block, there was a whinny. Amy looked up, expecting it to be Storm, but to her surprise it wasn't. It was Duke. He was looking at Ty.

"Wow!" Amy said, astounded.

"He's been doing really well," Ty said, going over to the big bay and patting him. "Daniel was right. There's not a mean bone in his body." Amy watched Ty stroke Duke's nose. "I'm pretty sure he must have been treated well by his previous owners," Ty continued, "and that his only bad experience was at Green Briar."

"Have you tried to pick his feet yet?" Amy asked.

"Not yet, but he'll let me touch his legs now," Ty said.

Just then, Ben came out of the tack room with Red's traveling blankets.

"Do you have a minute to help me load Red, Amy?" he asked, seeing her standing there.

"Sure," she replied.

Ben was going to a local show that afternoon. She unbolted the ramp. It felt kind of strange that she wasn't going, too, but at the same time she realized she felt a sense of relief. There was so much she wanted to do that afternoon — ride Dylan, groom Willow, spend some time with Sundance. She couldn't do any of it if she went to the show.

Ben led Red to the trailer. The handsome chestnut walked in eagerly, and Amy heaved the ramp into place.

"Good luck," she said as Ben let himself out the jockey door.

"It's only a small show," he said. "We're just going to have fun and get in some practice before Marriott Park." He looked up the yard. "Looks like someone else wants to come, too."

Amy followed his gaze. Storm was looking over his door. Nodding his head impatiently, he kicked his door, as if he were expecting to be loaded into the trailer, too.

"See you," Ben said to Amy and, getting into the pickup, he started the engine. As the trailer pulled away, Storm whinnied frantically.

Amy's heart clenched. It was obvious he wanted to go. He couldn't understand why he was being left behind.

"Hush now, boy," she said, going to his door. She stroked his face, but he pulled away from her, his eyes fixed on the trailer. As it disappeared from view he whinnied again and again, and nothing Amy did could soothe him.

She felt bad. She hated seeing him so upset.

"Storm, you can't go," she said. "We're not going to shows anymore."

Storm whinnied again, and the sound seemed to go

straight through Amy's heart. She couldn't bear to see him like this.

She looked toward the house and then headed for the phone.

❧

"You want me to ride Storm for you next Sunday?" Daniel echoed.

"Yes," Amy replied, her fingers gripping the receiver. "If you're free."

"I can do it, no problem," Daniel told her. "But I thought you said it wouldn't work, having someone else ride Storm in shows."

"It won't. It's just this once," Amy said. "I feel awful. Storm saw Red going off to a show just now and he keeps whinnying. He doesn't understand why he's been left behind. He's going to be just the same on Sunday when Ben goes to Marriott Park."

Daniel spoke slowly. "But what about the next time Ben goes to a show?"

Amy didn't want to think about it. "I'll think of something," she said. "I just need more time."

"OK," Daniel said. "Well, I'm more than happy to ride Storm for you. What's he entered in?"

"The High Juniors," Amy said. "I can call the show office and give them your name as his rider. You are still eighteen, aren't you?"

"Yes," Daniel replied. "So do you want me to come and pick up Storm in my trailer?"

"It's all right," Amy replied. "I'm sure Ben won't mind taking him with Red. He'll probably get there around nine."

"OK, tell him I'll meet him by the secretary's tent at nine-fifteen," Daniel said. "If he's going to be late he can call my cell phone." He paused. "You are sure about this, aren't you, Amy?"

"Yes," Amy insisted. She suddenly pictured Storm walking into the trailer, ready for the show, leaving her behind, and a tight band seemed to pull around her heart. She swallowed and forced the image away. "Yes," she repeated resolutely. "I'm sure."

Chapter Nine

On Sunday morning, Amy got up early to groom and braid Storm. "You be good, you hear?" she said as she led him out of his stall.

Storm watched Red load into the trailer. He pawed at the ground impatiently and pulled toward the ramp, his ears pricked. He looked so eager, so excited.

Amy swallowed. "I won't be there, Storm, but I'll be thinking about you," she told him. "Jump well for Daniel."

Storm snorted and pushed at her impatiently with his head.

"OK," Ben called.

Amy led Storm up the ramp. After tying him up, she gave him a last pat and slipped out through the jockey door. As she shut it, she saw Storm and Red touch noses as though they were pleased to be back together.

"Say good luck to Daniel for me," she said to Ben.

"I will," he promised, getting into the pickup.

Amy watched as he started the engine and drove away. With a sigh, she turned and trudged up the yard to continue mucking out.

She tried hard to keep herself busy, but she couldn't stop thinking about Storm. *He'll have arrived at the show now,* she thought, looking at her watch as she went into the straw barn. *Ben's probably just unloading him. He'll be looking around. The jumps will be out in the ring. . . .*

"Earth to Amy!" Lou waved a hand in front of her nose.

Amy jumped.

"That bale of straw's not going to get to the barn by itself," Lou commented.

"Sorry," Amy said, realizing that Lou was trying to get past her to pick up some clean straw.

"Thinking about Storm?" her sister asked.

Amy nodded and turned to pick up the bale.

"It must be tough for you." Lou spoke quietly. "But I do understand."

Amy stared.

"I know you think I don't love the horses like you do," Lou said, "and I guess I don't. But that doesn't stop me from being able to see what a difficult decision it must have been for you to give up showing. And I can guess how hard it must be for you to think of Storm competing with someone else."

Amy didn't know what to say. She hadn't admitted to anyone how much she hated the thought of Storm going to a show without her. She knew it made her sound selfish, and she was certain other people wouldn't understand. But Storm was just so precious to her.

"Look," Lou said gently, "what do you say we finish up the stalls and then take a drive to the show? It'll only take us twenty minutes by car. If we hurry we should get there in time to see Storm go in his class. We can come back immediately afterward, so we won't lose much time here."

A smile broke out on Amy's face. "I'd like that. Thanks, Lou."

Her sister smiled back. "No problem."

❧

They arrived at the show ground just after ten. The event was in full swing. Hurrying through the crowds of people, they headed for the jumper ring.

"And next in class thirty-one, we have number 266, Jane Simmons riding Hollow Whisper," the loudspeaker announced.

"That's my class," Amy said quickly.

"Look, there's Daniel!" Lou said, pointing to the warm-up ring.

As Amy's eyes fell on Storm, her heart seemed to miss a beat. Daniel was cantering him at one end of the ring. Storm's ears were pricked. Amy felt suddenly strange. It was harder than she thought it would be to see Storm there without her. He looked just like he always did at shows — he was in full form. *Well, how did you expect him to look?* she thought. Deep in her mind, she knew she'd wanted him to look different, to be less complete — to be missing her.

"Should we go and say hi?" Lou asked eagerly.

But suddenly Amy didn't want to. She shook her head. Seeing Lou's surprised expression, she said quickly, "It — it might upset Storm, it might make him lose focus."

Lou shrugged. "Well, you know Storm best. We can say hello afterward. Let's find a seat."

They sat down in the busy stands.

Amy hunched forward in her seat, her arms hugging her stomach. She didn't say anything. Her eyes stared at the ring, but she hardly even saw the horse that was jumping the course. All she could think about was Storm.

"That was four faults there for number 266, Jane Simmons on Hollow Whisper," the loudspeaker announced as the horse cantered out of the ring. There was a pause while the clapping died down, and then the loudspeaker crackled to life again. "Next in class thirty-one, number 125, Daniel Lawson riding Summer Storm."

Amy barely registered the polite clapping around her. Her eyes were fixed on Storm. He came trotting into the ring, his hooves flicking lightly across the grass, his head and neck flexed, his ears pricked in anticipation.

She saw Daniel lean forward on Storm's neck and murmur something. Storm's ears flickered, and he moved smoothly into his even-paced canter. Amy felt every hoofbeat, every stride of his powerful legs as he cantered around the ring.

The starting bell rang. Daniel stroked Storm's neck and then turned him toward the first fence. Storm's ears pricked, his stride lengthened, and they met it perfectly, flowing over it, moving as one.

Amy was spellbound. Lightly balanced on Storm's back, Daniel guided the gray gelding over jump after jump. They cleared each fence with inches to spare, and suddenly Amy could see what so many people had been telling her. Storm wasn't just good — she knew that from watching him jump at home with Daniel — he was breathtaking. Out of the showring he might be gentle and affectionate, but in the showring he became a different horse. Courage and strength seemed to shine out of his eager, willing eyes. He made you want to watch him. He made you believe he could jump the moon. And more than that, Amy suddenly saw what Ben and Daniel had been trying to tell her. Storm loved the ring. It was his home.

As Storm jumped the last fence of the jump-off course and galloped through the finish with the fastest clear round of the competition so far, the crowd erupted into loud applause. Grinning broadly, Daniel patted Storm's neck and slowed him down from a gallop into a canter and finally into a trot. Storm tossed his head with delight. He knew he'd done well.

"Amy."

Amy barely registered her sister's voice. She watched as Daniel rode out of the ring. She could see the exhilaration on his face, the happiness in Storm's eyes.

"Amy!" Lou put a hand on her arm. "Come on! Let's go find them. That round was amazing!"

Amy stood up as if in a dream. Her thoughts were spinning.

She followed Lou out of the stands toward the collecting ring. Suddenly, her heart clenched. There was Storm with Daniel. They looked so happy, so excited.

Amy stopped.

Lou looked at her. "What?" She seemed to see the paleness of Amy's face. "What is it?" she demanded.

Amy shook her head. "I — I can't," she said. "I can't see them."

"But why?" Lou asked.

Amy couldn't find the words. Her eyes begged Lou to understand.

Lou frowned in concern. "What's the matter?" she said solicitously.

Amy stared at Storm. "I just can't," she whispered. Her heart felt like it was going to break. Deep down, in the part of her that went beyond words, she knew what she was going to have to do. And she couldn't bear it.

"Please, Lou," she said, her voice trembling on the brink of tears. "I just want to go home."

To her relief, Lou didn't argue. She looked confused but she shrugged. "OK," she said as she started to turn for the parking lot.

"Amy! Lou!"

Amy's heart plummeted. It was too late. Ben had seen them.

"Over here!" he called.

Lou looked at Amy, wondering what to do. Amy swallowed. There was no way out now. Taking a deep breath, she forced her legs to move.

"Hi," she called. To her ears, her voice sounded forced and strange. But Ben and Daniel didn't seem to notice.

"It's good to see you!" Ben said as they walked over.

Storm nickered and raised his head.

"I didn't know you were coming to watch," Daniel said.

"It was an impulse decision," Lou said. Amy felt her

sister glance at her as if expecting her to say something, but Storm was nuzzling at her hands, and suddenly she found that she couldn't speak.

"We saw your round," Lou said quickly, as if to fill the silence. "It was amazing!"

Daniel grinned and patted Storm. "It didn't have anything to do with me. Storm is just brilliant!" He looked at Amy. "You can't be serious about not competing with him, Amy."

"I am," she said. She could feel tears prick at the back of her eyes, but no one seemed to notice.

"But he loves the ring," Daniel protested. "You can feel him change the second you ride through the gate. It's like he comes alive. You can't take that away from him."

"I know," Amy whispered. She stared at Storm's face, a lump swelling in her throat. She pushed the words painfully past it. "That's why" — she looked at Lou and took a deep breath — "that's why I think we should sell him."

"Sell him?" Ben echoed.

Feeling numb, Amy nodded. "If you agree, Lou," she said, her eyes on her sister's face.

Lou stared at her in astonishment.

"I don't understand," Daniel said quickly. "Why are you selling Storm?"

Amy turned to him. "You said it yourself, Daniel. You

said that Storm belongs in the showring. I saw that just now when you were riding him." She touched Storm's warm neck. "When Storm first came to Heartland, I promised that his happiness would always come first. If we keep him I'll be breaking that promise."

"So we sell him and you end up unhappy?" Lou said softly to her.

"If that's the way it has to be," Amy whispered toward the ground, blinking back the tears.

"But there are other options," Daniel said quickly. "Doing this — getting someone else to ride him in shows."

Amy was already shaking her head. "He deserves more than that. He needs someone who can spend time with him — at home and at shows. I can't give him the time he needs. Not with all the other horses there." Swallowing hard, she stroked Storm's face. "I wish I could, but I can't."

For a moment, no one spoke.

At last Ben sighed. "It's a big decision," he said.

Lou put an arm around Amy's shoulders. "Ben's right," she said quietly. "It is a big decision, but I'm sure it's for the best."

"What will you do?" Ben said. "Advertise him?"

"I guess," Amy replied. She hadn't thought that far. She looked at Lou. "I'll have to talk to Dad first. He might want to take him back."

"I don't think he will," Lou said. "He made it clear that Storm was a gift to us, but he might help us find a good home for him."

"I could spread the word around the show circuit if you want," Daniel said. "There'll be a lot of people interested in him."

Amy nodded wordlessly and, giving Storm one last pat, she turned and walked slowly to the car.

As Lou pulled the car up to the house, Amy realized she was going to have to face her decision, but she stayed in the car, staring distantly out the window. Lou sat with her, not knowing what to say.

After a moment, Ty seemed to realize something was wrong. He put down the water bucket he was carrying and hurried over.

Seeing Ty approach, Lou reached for the door handle. "I'll be in the house," she said, leaving Amy and Ty together.

Lou gave Ty a knowing nod, and he walked around to Amy's side of the car and opened the door. Kneeling down next to her, he searched her face in alarm. "Amy, what is it?" Ty said, his voice full of concern. "Has something happened to Storm?"

Amy shook her head. All the tears she had been holding back spilled from her eyes.

Ty's arms enfolded her. "Amy," he said as she began to cry, "what's wrong?"

"I don't want to sell him," she sobbed. "I don't want to."

"Sell who?" Ty questioned.

"Storm," Amy replied. "You should have seen him at the show. He looked so happy. It's not fair to keep him. He needs someone who can show him and give him all the attention he deserves. He can't stay here." Her voice choked on her tears. "I love him so much, Ty."

Ty kissed her hair. "I know you do," he said sadly. "So maybe selling him is for the best."

They sat there for half an hour, until Amy at last felt calm enough to think about the other horses. She set to work with a vengeance. She wanted to be busy. She wanted to have things to do to stop her thinking about Storm. Focusing intently on each task as she did it, she managed to push Storm to the back of her mind, but then Ben's trailer came up the drive.

As Ben lowered the ramp, Storm whinnied. When she saw his dark eyes and pricked ears, Amy's heart wanted to stop.

Ben handed his lead rope to Amy, along with a blue ribbon. "He won," he said.

Amy looked at the rosette for a moment, then handed

it back to Ben. "Daniel should have it." She swallowed hard and clicked her tongue. "Come on, Storm."

She led Storm to his stall. Touching his smooth shoulder, she tried to picture what it would be like to see him walking into a trailer as he left Heartland for the last time. How would she feel? But her mind went blank. It was as if she couldn't let herself imagine that. *This isn't happening*, she thought numbly. *This isn't real.*

🌿

Her sense of unreality continued. That evening she took the phone up to her room to make the phone call she'd been dreading.

"Amy," her dad said when he answered. "What a nice surprise!"

"Hi, Dad," Amy said quietly.

"How are you? Been up to anything exciting? How are Lou and Storm?"

"We're all fine." Amy hesitated. It was now or never. "Dad, I've — I've got something to tell you."

Her dad seemed to hear the seriousness in her voice. "What?"

"It's" — Amy paused — "it's Storm. Lou and I don't think we should keep him anymore." As the words came out she felt hollow inside.

Tim sounded shocked. "But why?"

Amy explained how she couldn't compete and run Heartland, about how she couldn't bear to see Storm unhappy, knowing it was her fault. "It's not fair," she finished. "He'll be happier with someone else. Lou agrees with me. It's not that I don't love him. I just love him too much to keep him." Tears sprang to her eyes. She blinked them away. "Would you like him back? We know how valuable he is. You could sell him."

"No. He's your horse — yours and Lou's," Tim said. "You've done all the work on him, and if you sell him, then you should keep the money. But are you sure that selling him is the right decision? There must be another way."

"There isn't," Amy told him. "This is the only way Storm'll be really happy. He needs an owner who has time for him — who can take him to shows and spoil him."

Her father tried to suggest possible solutions, but in the end he reluctantly had to agree that selling Storm seemed to be the only option. "Oh, Amy," he said, and she could hear the sadness in his voice. "I'd so hoped —"

His voice broke off, and Amy could hear him take a deep breath. "What matters is that you and Lou do what you think is best. Your happiness is very important to me."

Amy was sure he had been about to say he'd hoped to see her become a show jumper like he and her mom had been. She had hoped the same thing. "I'm sorry, Dad," she said, feeling as if she had somehow let him down.

"Amy, sweetheart," Tim said, "you have nothing to be sorry about. I know this must be really hard for you. But I gave Storm to you and Lou, and together you must decide what's best." He sighed. "Do you want me to help you find him a home?"

"Well, Daniel — my friend — is going to spread the word around the show circuit here," Amy said. "But if you hear of someone, I want Storm to go to a good home."

"I'll let you know right away," Tim promised.

"I'd better go now," Amy said quietly.

"OK," Tim replied. He paused. "Amy —"

"Yes?" she said.

"I love you very, very much," he said. "Whatever you do, whatever choices you make, that will never change."

"Thanks, Dad," Amy managed to say. "I love you, too. I'll speak to you soon."

Sinking down on the bed, she placed the phone down and put her head in her hands.

Chapter Ten

It's just a bad dream, Amy thought as she woke up the next morning. *Storm isn't really going.* But her relief was swiftly replaced by an icy coldness as she realized that it wasn't a dream. She really was going to sell Storm.

She lay in bed, wishing that time could stand still. But outside, the horses were already starting to kick at their stall doors. She had to get up. They needed their breakfast.

Amy dressed slowly. As she went outside, Ty pulled up in front of the house in his pickup.

"How are you today?" he asked, looking at her with concern.

Amy shrugged. "I've been better."

Ty nodded understandingly. "Do you want to talk about it?"

Amy shook her head. There was nothing to say. She looked at the stable block and saw Storm looking at her. She swallowed and looked away.

Ty put an arm around her shoulders. "Come on," he said quietly. "Let's feed the horses."

Amy was in the middle of mucking out Jake's stall when the phone rang. She ran to the house to answer it.

"Heartland, Amy Fleming speaking," she said, her mind still half on the yard, thinking about what there was to do.

"Hi," a man said curtly. "My name's Buchanan, Charles Buchanan. I believe you have a horse for sale. A gray gelding? Jumps in Juniors?"

For a moment, Amy was almost too shocked to speak. "Um — yes," she said. She collected herself quickly. "We haven't advertised him yet."

"I was at Marriott Park yesterday. I heard the guy riding him talking to some people. He said he was for sale."

"Yes, well, yes, he is," Amy said, feeling slightly unnerved.

"Great," the man said. "I've seen him jump several times. He's a talented horse. I should think several of my clients would be interested in buying him."

"Clients?" Amy said.

"I'm a horse dealer," Mr. Buchanan said. "How much are you asking for him?"

Amy didn't know what to say. She hadn't even thought of a price. All she'd thought about was getting Storm a good home. "You're a dealer?"

"Yes, that's right," Mr. Buchanan said. "What price do you want?"

"I'm sorry." Amy felt awkward, but it was Storm's happiness that was at stake. "But he's not for sale to a dealer. I want to know what kind of home he's going to."

"I'll pay you cash," Mr. Buchanan said.

"It doesn't matter," Amy said firmly. "Finding him a good home is more important to us than money. I'm sorry."

She replaced the receiver. She couldn't believe they'd had a call about Storm already. She'd have to talk to Lou about what price they were going to ask for him. She felt sick at the thought. All she wanted was for Storm to be happy.

⁋

By mid-morning, three more people had telephoned about Storm. All of them had been unsuitable as far as Amy was concerned. Two of them had been dealers like Mr. Buchanan, and one had been the father of a young rider who had a string of six horses.

"I don't want you to go to someone who already has a bunch of horses that are just exercised by stable hands," she told Storm. "You deserve a home where there'll be someone who'll spend time with you — who'll really love you."

He snorted and lowered his face so she could scratch his forehead.

"You big softy," Amy told him, rubbing his head.

She looked at Ty. He was working with Duke in the yard.

Duke's ears flickered nervously, but he stood still as Ty ran a hand down his legs.

"He's looking good," Amy commented.

Ty nodded. "I want to try picking up one of his feet. Would you hold him for me? I don't want to keep him tied in case he freaks out. Being tied would just upset him more."

"Sure." Amy went over and untied Duke.

"That's a good boy," Ty said, patting him. "Now, let's just have a look at this foot." Running his hand down Duke's left foreleg, he clicked his tongue and leaned his weight slightly against Duke's shoulder. Duke raised his head anxiously, but then he lifted his hoof just as Ty wanted.

"Good boy!" Ty exclaimed, holding the toe of the hoof just an inch or so off the ground.

Amy patted the gelding in delight.

Putting Duke's hoof down, Ty fed him a chunk of carrot. "Well, that seemed to go OK," he said. "I'll try a hind leg now."

Slowly, he worked his way around the horse's other three hooves.

With every minute that passed, Duke seemed to relax more, and soon he was willingly lifting all his hooves for Ty.

After Ty had worked his way around Duke's hooves twice and picked them clean, he stopped and frowned. "Something's not right, Amy."

"What do you mean?" she asked curiously.

Ty looked at Duke. "I don't understand why he was so bad at Green Briar. I mean, look at him now. He's lifting all his feet just fine. If he had been acting up because he had been genuinely scared, then there's no way it would be this easy. If he were stressed I'd have stopped after lifting one hoof a tiny way off the ground. But he's fine with me picking his feet up."

"That's true," Amy said, understanding what he was getting at. She looked at Duke's relaxed face. "He doesn't seem fazed at all."

"It all started when the farrier came, didn't it?" Ty asked.

Amy nodded. "Are you thinking he might be scared of being shod?"

"Maybe," Ty said. He frowned. "But then that wouldn't explain why he kept acting up when the farrier wasn't there."

"And the farrier didn't actually shoe him," Amy said, remembering what Daniel had told her. "He only got as far as lifting his foot onto the stand when Duke freaked." An idea came to her. "Maybe he's scared of the stand."

Ty didn't look convinced. "No, then he would have been fine once the farrier left."

"I guess so," Amy said, realizing he was right.

"Hang on," Ty said suddenly. "It could have something to do with lifting his foot onto the stand, though. Let's see."

He ran his hand down one of Duke's forelegs. Duke obediently picked up his hoof.

Keeping an eye on Duke's face, Ty slowly pulled the horse's leg out to the front just as a farrier would do and started to lift it as if he were about to place the hoof on a stand.

Duke immediately flung his head up, his muscles tensing in pain.

Instantly, Ty eased Duke's foot back to the ground. "It's OK, boy."

Amy looked at Ty. "It hurts! That's what it is."

"He doesn't seem to have any particularly sore spots," Ty said, his fingers gently examining Duke's forelegs, chest, and shoulders. The gelding didn't flinch. "It seems to only be when his foot is lifted out at that angle."

Amy thought back. "Could it have anything to do with the way Val Grant rushed him back into work?" she suggested. "Maybe it made those muscles sore."

Ty nodded. "I think I'll give Scott a call and see what he thinks." He patted Duke. "We'll figure it out, Duke. Don't worry."

❧

Amy put Duke away in his stall while Ty phoned the vet.

She was refilling Duke's water bucket when Ty came out of the house. "What did he say?" she asked.

"He's going to stop by tomorrow, but he suggested it might be a good idea to get a chiropractor to see him," Ty replied.

"Does he know one?" Amy asked.

"Yes, he gave me the name of a friend of his — Dr. Max Barker."

"Are you going to call him?" Amy asked.

"I called him, and he said he'll be in the area this afternoon. He can stop by after lunch."

❧

Dr. Barker arrived just after two o'clock. He was a tall, thin man in his forties with a wide smile and thinning hair. Dressed in jeans, a T-shirt, and gym shoes, he didn't look much like a horse vet, but as soon as he started working on Duke it was clear he knew exactly what he was doing.

He asked them what they knew about Duke's history and then watched the bay gelding's movement as he trotted on the lunge. "OK, that's enough," he said, nodding. "I'll just check him over."

Ty stroked Duke's face while the chiropractor rubbed and pressed different points on Duke's back, hindquarters, shoulders, and neck. Throughout the process, there was a quizzical look on his face.

Within five minutes, he started to nod to himself.

"OK," he said at last, finishing his examination and patting Duke. "He's sore in his shoulders, withers, and through his neck. His hips are a little inflamed, too. From what you've told me, I'd say that the sudden onset of exercise after a prolonged layoff caused most of his problems." He shook his head. "You can't expect a horse to come back to full work in a matter of weeks."

"Can you do anything to help him?" Amy asked.

"Sure," Dr. Barker said. "I'd say three or four sessions over the next few weeks should do it."

"It'll make him better?" Ty said.

Dr. Barker nodded. "Should make him as good as new, as long as his exercise schedule is slow and steady."

Amy and Ty exchanged delighted glances.

Dr. Barker patted Duke. "Come on, boy, let's get started."

He began to gently manipulate Duke's neck and withers with his hands, rubbing his muscles at different angles.

"I can't believe all Duke's problems were caused by Val," Amy said in disgust. "And yet I can believe it. That woman has no regard for anything — unless it benefits her in the end."

"Duke must have been so sore from the work that it killed him when the farrier tried to lift up his leg," Ty said. "He was forcing already tender muscles to stretch in an unnatural way. No wonder Duke freaked out."

"And that's why he reacted whenever anyone tried picking up his legs after that," Amy said.

"Poor guy," Ty said, stroking Duke's face. "You were just trying to say you were in pain, and you ended up getting beaten for it. I would have resorted to biting and kicking, too."

Dr. Barker looked up. "It's unbelievable how many stubborn or bad horses are really just in pain," he said. "Their attitude is a defense mechanism, an attempt to protect themselves."

Amy nodded. She had seen it over and over again at Heartland — horses being labeled as difficult, when really they were trying to let someone know that they were hurting or frightened. "I wish people listened more to what horses are trying to say," she said wistfully.

Dr. Barker nodded in agreement. "But then I see

places like yours," he said, looking around at Heartland, "and that gives me hope. We can make a difference — those of us who care. No matter how small, it is a difference."

Amy smiled. She liked Dr. Barker more with every minute.

"OK, then, all done," he said at last. "I'll come back in two days for Duke's next treatment. All right with you?"

"That's great," Amy said. "Thank you."

While Ty put Duke away in his stall, Amy walked to Dr. Barker's car with him. "See you on Wednesday," she called as he got into his Jeep and drove away.

Amy was about to go back to Duke's stall when she stopped in her tracks. A silver car was coming up the drive — a very smart Mercedes. Amy frowned. She knew that car. Whose was it? She stared. It was the Grants'!

Amy watched in astonishment as Val drove until the car was about three feet away from her and stopped the engine.

Ashley was sitting in the passenger seat. She didn't get out. She didn't even look in Amy's direction.

Val Grant opened her door. "Hello, Amy." She smiled.

Something inside Amy immediately trembled with distrust. Why did Val insist on acting like they were friends?

"What do you want, Mrs. Grant?" she asked.

Val Grant got out of the car. "I was wondering if either your sister or grandfather were around."

"No, they're not. They're both out," Amy said.

"That's too bad." Val gave a slight shake of her head. "Well," she said, "maybe you can help. I hear Storm's for sale."

Amy stared at her.

"I'd be interested in buying him," Val continued briskly. "That's why I wanted to see your sister or grandfather. To discuss a reasonable price. You've done quite well with him, considering."

"Considering what?" Amy demanded.

"Well" — Val looked around meaningfully at Heartland's barns and fields — "this isn't exactly the place for a horse of Storm's abilities, is it, Amy? Even you can see that. He's got real talent. He can't be properly challenged here."

A wave of anger rose up inside Amy. "So you think he'd be better off with you?" she said.

Val raised her eyebrows and cocked her head to the side. "Well, obviously. We have the best training facility in the state — and we could match Storm with a rider of comparable talent."

Amy wasn't sure if she was more infuriated or amused. Struggling to control herself, she said coldly, "I think you should leave now, Mrs. Grant. We're not going to sell Storm to you."

"I see." Val smiled at Amy as if she were a child. "Look, maybe I should be discussing this with your grandfather."

"The answer will still be no," Amy said. "I have the final say on where Storm goes."

"I'm willing to pay a very good price," Val said.

Amy couldn't believe that Val didn't get it. "It doesn't matter how much you offer," she said. "There's no way I'm selling him to you."

At that moment, Duke put his head over his stall door.

Val stared as if she couldn't believe her eyes. "That horse!" she exclaimed, momentarily forgetting about Storm. "What's he doing here? I sold him to Daniel Lawson!"

"Yes. Daniel bought him for us," Amy said. "We're helping him."

Val Grant snorted in disbelief. "Then you're even more foolish than I thought. You can't help him. He's crazy. Take my advice — what he needs is a bullet through the head."

Amy finally snapped. "What he needs is someone who is patient. Who will take the time to understand his pain!" she said furiously. "The only reason Duke acted up is because his muscles are so sore it hurts for his feet to be picked up. And the reason he is that sore is because of how you worked him at Green Briar. You can't bring him back to full work in two weeks. Didn't you think he might feel sore? Didn't you think to check?"

She saw Val's initial surprise turn to anger. "You think you've got it all figured out, don't you?" Val demanded. "You know nothing about what I did with that horse. About how I tried to cure him."

"By shooting him with a pellet gun?" Amy said. "That's just one of the reasons I wouldn't sell Storm to you. Just one. He deserves more than a good facility and a skilled rider, but you wouldn't understand that."

Val Grant's face stiffened. She stared at Amy for a moment and then swung around and walked back to her car.

In the middle of shutting her car door, Val stopped. "You can be as high and mighty as you like, Amy Fleming, but when that horse leaves here you've got no say over his future. No say at all."

She slammed the car door shut and drove away. Ashley hadn't looked at Amy once.

Amy stared after them as the truth in Val's last words sank in. Once Storm left Heartland, she would have no say in his life. Show horses were bought and sold all the time. What if he ended up in a bad home?

She walked up to Storm's stall and looked over his door. He was lying down. He nickered softly when he saw her.

Amy went into the stall and knelt down beside him. He nuzzled her knees, and she felt a wave of despair sweep over her. "I don't know what to do," she whispered, feeling suddenly panicked. "I just don't know what to do."

The phone started to ring. Knowing that Ty and Ben were in the far pastures, Amy kissed Storm and reluctantly got up. She didn't feel like answering the phone. It would probably just be another phone call about Storm, but it might be an emergency — someone who knew about a horse that needed their help. She couldn't ignore it.

She ran to the house and picked up the phone.

"Hi, Amy."

She immediately recognized the voice of Nick Halliwell.

"Nick, hi!" Amy spoke with a rush of relief when she realized that it wasn't another call about Storm.

"You sound like you're having a good day," Nick said, sounding surprised.

"Not really. It's just I thought you were going to be another person calling about Storm," Amy explained. "It's been overwhelming."

"Well," Nick said, "actually, that *is* why I'm calling. Have you sold him yet?"

Amy frowned in confusion. "No. Why?"

"Because I'd like to buy him."

Amy was too shocked to speak.

"Amy?" Nick said when she didn't say anything.

"You want to buy Storm?" Amy stammered.

"Definitely," Nick replied. "I think he's got tremendous talent and ability. I'd love the chance to work with him."

"You'd show him — in jumpers?" Amy asked.

"No." Nick's voice had a smile in it. "I'd take him in barrel-racing competitions. What do you think, Amy? Of course I'd jump him."

"But — well, I just never expected it," she stammered.

"I mean I wouldn't jump him that much to start," Nick said. "I'm often away at shows, so I trust my students to train the young horses to some extent. Each working pupil has two or three horses, and they consult me about the horses' progress."

"Yes, I know," Amy said, remembering her conversation with Daniel.

"I heard how well he jumped for Daniel yesterday," Nick continued. "And what I'd like to do, if I do buy Storm, is to make Daniel his designated rider. He'd be in charge of schooling him and taking him in shows. He'd stay with him as he moves up through the divisions. I know they'd become a great team."

The memory of Daniel patting Storm's neck at the show flashed into Amy's mind. Then she thought of the bond Daniel had shared with his horse, Amber, and she knew he would be just as devoted to Storm.

Amy could hardly contain her delight. "I would really like that, and I think Storm would, too."

"That's great," Nick said. "So I guess the question is how much are you asking for him?"

Amy hesitated. "I'd like to talk to Lou about it, and she's not here now."

"That sounds fine," Nick said. "I can wait. So you'll consider selling him to me?"

"Yes," Amy said. Then a thought returned to her — an important one. "You won't sell him? Will you, Nick? I really want Storm to have a good home."

Nick paused. "I can't guarantee that I'll keep him forever," he said honestly. "I don't have space for horses that don't reach their potential."

"Oh," Amy said, feeling her excitement deflate slightly. It had all seemed so perfect.

"But," Nick went on, "I'm sure we could come to some agreement where I could let you buy him back if I ever do decide to sell him."

Amy felt a wave of relief. "I'll have to discuss it with Lou and Grandpa," she said. "But I think that sounds great."

As if on cue, she heard Grandpa and Lou arrive home with the groceries. "May I call you back in about ten minutes?" she asked Nick.

"Sure," he said.

❧

"So what do you think?" she asked Grandpa and Lou after she'd told them about Nick's offer.

Grandpa sat down at the table. "It sounds good," he said.

"And Nick's so nice," Lou said. "It would be great for Storm to go to a show-jumping home like that — and to have Daniel look after him."

Amy nodded. She knew Daniel would take care of Storm as if he were his own horse.

"I think it's a great idea," Lou said. "And he wouldn't be too far away."

"I'll go and call Nick back. And make sure the price is OK," Amy said. She went into the office and punched in Nick's number.

He answered the phone almost immediately. He was delighted when he heard the news. "That's great," he said. "In that case, I'll send Daniel over for him as soon as possible."

Amy felt a shock run through her. This was real. Storm was actually going to leave Heartland. Daniel was going to come and load him up and take him away.

"Would tomorrow morning be good?" Nick continued. "I'm leaving for a show in Germany on Wednesday, and I'd really like to be here when he arrives."

Amy felt sick. "Yes," she heard herself saying. "Yes, tomorrow morning would be fine."

"Great," Nick said. "Daniel will be there about ten."

Amy slowly put the phone down. She went into the kitchen and looked at Grandpa and Lou in a daze.

"Are you OK?" Lou asked.

"Daniel's coming for Storm tomorrow morning," Amy said. Her words sounded strange and distant, almost as if someone else were speaking them.

"That soon?" Grandpa said, surprised.

Lou came over to her. "I'm sure Nick will understand if you want to keep Storm a couple of weeks longer," she said, looking at her sympathetically.

"It's OK," Amy said. "I — I said it's fine."

She left the kitchen and walked outside. Hearing her footsteps, Storm came to his door and whinnied.

"Hey, boy," she whispered. She went over to him, her eyes scanning every inch of his handsome face. She loved him so much, and tomorrow he was going away. She rested her forehead against his nose. He snorted softly. She stood there for a moment, and then, taking a deep breath, she forced herself to head up the yard to tell Ty and Ben the news.

They were in the feed room, measuring out the evening grain.

"He'll be good for Daniel," Ben said when she told them about Nick's phone call.

Amy nodded wordlessly.

"And you'll be able to visit Storm a lot," Ben added.

Amy inwardly flinched. *Visit Storm* . . .

"How are you feeling about it?" Ty asked her.

Amy nodded. "OK," she said, her voice high and tight. "I — I'm OK." She hesitated. "I think I'll go and start sweeping the yard," she said.

She walked off. The world seemed slightly blurred, as if she were somehow out of rhythm — like it was moving without her. Picking up a yard brush, she began to sweep.

&

After everyone had gone that night, Amy took Storm's bridle from the tack room. She brushed him over and saddled him without a word. Seeming to sense something was wrong, Storm nuzzled her arm as she put the reins over his head.

She couldn't think of anything to say. She stroked his face.

Tomorrow, she thought, but she couldn't think beyond that.

Feeling empty inside, she led him out of the stall and mounted. The evening sunlight was soft, and birds sang in the branches of the nearby trees. Not to ride Storm again, not to see him in his stall, not to hear his whinny. Life would be different after tomorrow.

Shortening her reins, she rode him out onto the trail

that led up the hillside behind Heartland. He walked out, his stride swinging, his ears pricked.

As the trail entered the trees, Amy let him move into a trot and then a canter. She leaned forward, feeling his powerful muscles move beneath her, feeling the wind in her face, and, suddenly, she was filled with the desire to ride him on and on, far away from Heartland and the coming morning.

On and on, she thought as his hooves thudded rhythmically into the grass. Her mind cleared as, for one blissful moment in time, she let herself believe it. *On and on. Forever.*

Where the trail started twisting and turning, Storm slowed down. And as he did so, reality flooded back. Amy pulled him to a walk and sadly patted his neck, acknowledging what she knew. There was not going to be a forever for her and Storm.

❧

Amy slept badly that night. She got up early and was already feeding the horses when Ty arrived.

"Look, why don't you spend time with Storm this morning?" Ty said to her. "Ben and I can do the stalls."

"I can help, too."

Amy turned. Lou was coming out of the house, her short blond hair still ruffled from sleep. "Ty's right," Lou said. "You should be with Storm."

"Thanks," Amy said quietly.

She grabbed Storm's grooming kit and halter and set to work brushing him. She felt as if all her actions were slower than normal. *This is the last time,* she thought with every brush stroke, *the last time I'll be grooming him.*

But there was a bit of her that didn't quite believe it. And it wasn't until Nick's trailer came rattling up the drive that, finally, Amy knew it was true.

"Amy," Daniel said, getting out of the pickup and coming to meet her.

"Hi," she said in a small voice.

Daniel's eyes searched her face. "I don't know what to say. I'm really happy that Nick's buying Storm, but I know it can't be easy for you."

"I'd rather Nick and you had him than anyone else," Amy said.

Their eyes met.

"I'll — I'll go get him ready," Amy said.

"Amy, wait," Daniel said as she set off to the tack room. "Nick sent some travel blankets. He thought it would save bringing yours back."

"Oh, right," Amy said, stopping.

Daniel pulled the wraps from the truck cab. "Do you want a hand?"

Amy shook her head.

"I'll go and say hi to the others," Daniel said understandingly. "Just give a shout when you're ready."

Amy walked slowly up to Storm's stall. Seeing the wraps in her arms, he nickered excitedly. Amy felt her heart twist. "You're not going to a show, boy," she said.

But Storm didn't understand. He pawed the ground eagerly.

Taking a deep breath, Amy crouched down and began to fasten Nick's wraps.

All too soon, Storm was ready.

"I'm done," Amy said as she straightened up after closing the last Velcro strap. Her throat felt tight. She walked over to Storm's head and kissed his face. For a moment she closed her eyes. "I'm doing this for you," she whispered. "For you, Storm."

Taking a deep breath, she opened her eyes and went to the door. "Daniel!" she called, trying to keep her voice steady. "Storm's ready to go."

She went back to Storm and untied him. "I love you," she told him desperately. "Just remember that. No one could ever love you more." Hot tears filled her eyes.

Hearing footsteps in the yard, she quickly brushed them away and, swallowing hard, she led Storm out of his stall.

"Hi, Storm," Daniel said, patting him.

Ben, Ty, and Lou came over.

"You be good for Daniel, Storm," Lou said to the gray gelding.

"Just don't go beating me and Red in any shows," Ben said, rubbing the gelding's face.

"Bye, Storm," Ty said softly.

Daniel glanced at Amy. "Do you want to take him into the trailer?"

Amy hesitated. "You do it," she said, handing over the lead rope.

Daniel took it, and Storm walked forward eagerly as Amy stood and watched.

When Storm reached the trailer, Amy couldn't bear it any longer. She ran forward, placing a hand on his withers and wrapping the other around his neck.

"Amy?" Daniel said.

She buried her head against Storm. *I can't,* she thought desperately. *I can't let him go.* Just then, Storm stepped eagerly toward the trailer.

Pulling away, Amy looked at his pricked ears. She drew in a trembling breath and slowly took her hand from his neck.

"Love him for me, Daniel," she pleaded, her voice barely a whisper.

"I will," Daniel said, holding her gaze.

Amy stepped away. Her jaw ached with the effort of holding back all the emotion inside, all the things she wanted to say.

"I'll call when we get to Nick's," Daniel said quietly as he put the ramp up.

Amy nodded.

The trailer drove slowly away, and a tear trickled

down her cheek, then another. She heard footsteps behind her, and she felt Ty take her hand.

"You did the right thing," he told her, his fingers gripping hers.

Amy shook her head wordlessly, her face now streaming with tears.

"Look around you, Amy," Ty said.

Amy glanced around the yard, wondering what she was supposed to be looking at. Lou and Ben were standing by Willow, who reached her head over the paddock fence. In the distance, the other horses and ponies were grazing in the fields.

"You couldn't have given this up," Ty said. "I know losing Storm is hard, Amy, but you'll still be able to see him. Giving up Heartland would have meant giving up your heart."

A sob burst from Amy, and she buried her head against his chest. She knew Ty was right but, just at that moment, she couldn't think of anything but Storm.

Wrapping his arms around her, Ty let her cry for all she had lost.

Her sobs gradually quieted down, and Amy lifted her head. As she looked again at the sunny yard and the peaceful horses, Ty kissed her forehead. In that instant, she knew that she had made the right choice — for Storm, for the horses that needed her at Heartland, and for herself.

Looking around Heartland, she saw her future.

"Everything will be OK," Ty whispered, taking her hand.

Amy smiled through her tears. "I know," she said, and, in her heart, she meant it.

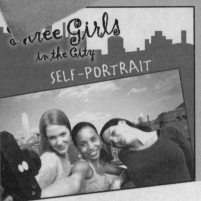